Maye West M

Options B

By
Brenda Colbath

OPTIONS

First edition. November 12, 2023.

ISBN: 979-8223010890

Written by Brenda Colbath.

Also by Brenda Colbath

Book 1
Spirited One

Maye West Murder Mysteries
Murder on Lake Haverly
Options

The Spirited One
James Book 2

Dedication:

This book is dedicated to my Husband, Shirl, in honor of his suffering through reading scripts each time I "revised." His encouragement kept me going every time I quit.

Thank you, Dawnzella, my daughter, for taking my idea of what I wanted for the cover of this book and creating a perfect finished product.

Chris, my son, for always being available for help with word, and thinking I write great complaint letters. Including the one when he was kicked off the school bus that got him riding again.

Thanks to the Weller family for their encouragement allowing me to publish a series of books with their family as the main characters!

And finally, for my teacher at Corinna Union Academy. He insisted that we write five pages of handwritten "Random Notes" weekly. He significantly impacted my life, and I loved tantalizing him with "continued" stories.

Other books by Brenda Colbath

Murder on Lake Haverly Book: 1 Maye West Mysteries

Options Book: 2 Maye West Mysteries

Immortal Enemies

Spirited One

The end of the Road

Ruby & Nolan's Great Adventures in Space Book: 1 The Science Project

Ruby & Nolan's Great Adventures in Space Book: 2 Dragon Flight

Ruby & Nolan's Great Adventures in Space Book: 3 The Keep

Ruby & Nolan's Great Adventures in Space Book: 4 The Others

Ruby & Nolan's Great Adventures in Space Book: 5 Wormhole

Ruby & Nolan's Great Adventures in Space Book: 6 Merpeople

Ruby & Nolan's Great Adventures in Space Book:7 Decisions

Sleep Travelers Book: 1 The Story of Ning, Dog, & Boss

Sleep Travelers Book2: The Amusement Park

Chapter 1 Money isn't Everything!

Mucho Dinero was sticking out of my files, but none of those deals were mine: Dammit! My personal production was below zero! I know what you are thinking! The hundreds of West Real Estate signs all over Maricopa County should make me happy!

I kept reminding myself of the mountains of Broker-stuff I have to do. I was juggling too many balls, but those weren't the ones I longed to juggle. Frank Singleton, my long-time best friend with benefits, was out of town attending a month-long conference, and I was missing him more than I wanted to admit.

Shaking myself out of my funk, I forced my mind to create two full-color pages of advertising copy for Homes Illustrated. My agents were running ragged listing and selling properties; the least I could do was write ads designed to make their phones ring. The hours of creating advertising copy got my mind off the desire for some much-needed alone time with Frank. Almost!

I focused on planning an Open House, giving me some much-needed busy work. Cards, signs, balloons, and a helium canister were on my shortlist. The smell of baking cinnamon rolls gets the juices flowing and the home fires burning. When customers hold a warm role or two in their hands, they stay long enough to eat them!

A picture of other hot buns belonging to Frank popped into my mind, and I started falling head over heels down that rabbit hole of depression. The ringing of the phone saved me from smashing head-first onto rock bottom. "West Realty, Maye speaking," I said, putting a cheerful sound in my voice I did not feel.

"Hi, Maye, I have the weekend free. Have you got anything going?" Frank asked.

"Are you kidding? I have been up to my ears in book work; the kids are busier than one-armed paperhangers. Lavonne is in Texas for a month. Help! How soon can you get here?" I asked, running my sentences together, not taking a breath.

"Hang in there! I am pulling into town and have reservations at that new hotel in Avondale. How fast can you pack?"

"Are you kidding? I'll be ready in 20 minutes, no, make that 10! On second thought, drive by the office, peep the horn, open the door, and I will run and jump in."

"Maye, what's got you so riled?"

"I am so bored; I could spit! I haven't had a sale for so long; I don't know if I can remember how to write a contract! Today, I am over-planning an open house for a listing that isn't even mine!" I said, running my hand through my now messy, curly, red hair. I had been sweating, creating the advertising; my minimal makeup was now decorating my chest.

"Hang on, Hon! I will be there in a few minutes to break you out of prison," he said, laughing as he hung up.

After locking the office and placing a "gone fishing" sign on the door, I ran upstairs, giving my heart some much-needed cardio exercise. I stumbled into my apartment and discovered a tornado had struck. "Good God, I can't let Frank see this mess," I muttered, turning into a Tasmanian cleaning Devil. Frank knocked minutes later, and I reluctantly let him in. He folded into his arms, kissing my forehead and holding me for several minutes. It was pure heaven!

I looked up into his handsome face, his pale blue eyes showing empathy; I couldn't wait to be naked in his arms. We yanked his civvies off in seconds; my t-shirt and shorts followed. I jumped into his arms, wrapping my legs around his tall, slim body, showing how happy he was to be with me. We kiss-walked and fell into my unmade bed, and after the quick, hard, fast sex we both needed, we came up for air.

Frank suggested I pack while he confirmed reservations! I threw several things in a bag, combed my hair, washed my face, added lip gloss, and away we flew.

Our romantic suite had a view of the White Tank Mountains, a cloud-soft king-size bed, and a Jacuzzi tub with Red Rose petals and candles. I slid into the soft scented water, and Frank massaged the tight muscles of my neck. I closed my eyes, relaxing until the water became cold. Magically, Frank appeared again, wrapping me in a big thirsty towel, and left while I dried my body and my hair. I slipped into a sexy negligee and, upon entering the room, found dinner waiting with champagne.

For the next two days, we dined and made sweet love. Our idyllic weekend was over in an instant, and we went our separate ways with smiles on our faces.

Back to business! I borrowed one of my Agent's listings on 3825 West Columbus Drive in West Peoria. It was in a 55+ subdivision surrounding the clubhouse. The formal yet homey atmosphere was complemented by its spacious kitchen, featuring marble-top counters and stainless steel appliances. A banquet-sized formal dining room with a dance hall-sized living room added the finishing touches. The side entrance, partially hidden behind a three-car garage, ensured privacy to this single-story stucco with a concrete shingle roof covered with solar panels overlooking a tiny backyard.

There is safety in numbers when holding vacant houses open. Security has never been one of my concerns; my Glock26 rests comfortably in my fanny pack riding on my left hip. Although it is acceptable to open carry in Arizona, clients are a little shy of Realtors toting a gun. I practice safe Real Estate! It's not smart to park in the driveway when showing vacant homes; a mister-friendly rapist might park behind you, thus cutting off your best avenue of escape.

After setting up my display in the lovely dining room, I popped the cinnamon rolls in the oven, turned on all the lights, opened the blinds, added several cases of bottled water in the fridge and an opened bag of ice in the freezer.

Staying hydrated in the desert is mandatory, and I learned the hard way to never drink alcohol when working! Sandy McClusky, a kick-in-the-pants Broker, trained me how, or rather how not, to hold an Open House!

Sandy and I were hot, bored, and thirsty and drank several Almaden Mountain Rhine glasses over ice. Not a single person showed up until late in the day. We jumped up with big smiles on our faces, ready to greet our one and only hot prospect! I still cringe, remembering neither of us coming close to acting professional and sober. We didn't sell the house. Lesson learned! Come to think of it, I learned most lessons the hard way.

Back to my present Open House! After checking and re-checking everything, I paced the floor, waiting for the hordes of customers to fall all over themselves, bidding on this jewel. Yeah Right!

I was about to give up the ghost, thinking it was a wash when three young men walked in. Handing a card and flyer to each of them, I said, "Hello, I am Maye West. Would you like a tour of the house?"

The tallest one said, "Hello, Maye, my name is Nathanial Harris, but my friends call me Nate." Taking the flyer and card, he didn't introduce his friends.

Nate was slim, towering above me, and appeared in his late twenties, with a short Afro, big brown eyes, dark skin, and a big, friendly smile. He took the seat opposite me.

He said, "Thanks, but I'm not interested in this house. It's beautiful, but the one I want is a few blocks from here. Would you be interested in writing up the deal for me?"

"*Hot Damn, does a chicken have lips?*" My mood lightened considerably.

"Nate, I will be glad to help you purchase any house you want."

"This will be an easy sale for you! The seller and I have already agreed on the price! I am going to give her $30,000.00 and take over her payments." Nate said, his big smile dazzling me.

"Unfortunately, Nate, that isn't how it's done! The bank will require you to qualify for a new loan."

Immediately, Nate's face fell, "Well, you can rite a contract around hers, can't you? I am pretty sure I can't qualify for a loan. I have a chair in my wife's Barber/Hair Stylist shop and do handyman work."

Sensing he was about to bolt, I placed my hand on his arm. "Wait a minute, Nate, let's talk; I know a way to get you into that house legally, and it won't require a credit report or a Bank!"

He shrugged, "Okay, but I've gotta have to have that house! My baby girl, Amanda, needs a yard to play in."

"Relax, Nate, first, a short history lesson. Banks wrote an alienation clause in their mortgages in 1980. That gives the mortgage company the right to call the note, making the balance due and payable immediately when a contract is written around the mortgage. The Banks have the money, so we must play by their rules! I promise I will get you into that house legal and properly!"

"Okay, but how are you going to do that?" He said, settling back in his chair.

"Listen carefully, Nate. We will write a lease contract with an option-greement, and you will have two years to exercise your option to purchase the property with a bank loan. Your option money will be forfeited to the seller, which you were going to do, anyway. Your down payment will be the option money and a portion of the rent."

"That all sounds great, but the seller can't come back to town to sign papers."

"That is not a problem; the papers can be signed by mail. Why can't the seller come back?"

"Her ex-husband is crazy jealous and is pissed that she put him in prison for beating her to a pulp! He threatened to kill her and anyone who helped her when he got out. She can't let anyone know where she is hiding!"

"Don't worry, Viv Appleton, my friend at Capitol Title, and my attorney will help me put this together. No one needs to know the seller's address. Nate, this is important to you: she won't be able to stop the sale even if she wanted to!"

Nate sat up straight in his chair with a big shit-eating grin on his face, and for a minute, I thought he was going to hug me; instead, we high-fived.

"What do you need from me?" he asked.

"I need you to take me to the house tomorrow at 8:00 Am. Is it vacant? Do you have keys?"

"Yes, it is, and I do have the keys."

"Good; after I tour the house and write a listing, we will meet with Viv at Capitol Title and take care of the paperwork. You will need to bring your option money check with you."

"Thank you for not blowing me off like the other agents; I will pick you up at your office at 8:00!" Nate shook my hand, making it look tiny, encased in his. With a big smile, he grabbed several cinnamon buns and ushered his friends out the door.

I sat back in my chair, a big smile on my face! Finally, the dam broke! You need what Realtors call "easy" deals to keep the door open and the lights on. The difficult ones get your juices flowing, and man, my juices were flowing like a tsunami tide!

The next morning, Nate and I toured the house at 4836 W. Columbine Ave; it was a real beauty! It sat on a one hundred by one hundred foot fenced lot with an adequately fenced pool. This mini-mansion was close to 5,000 square feet with four large bedrooms: three up and one down. I joked about the "Harry Potter closet under the stairs, and Nate said, "It will be perfect for my safe." I thought, *"Why in the world does he need a safe that big? Oh well, to each his own!"*

The kitchen would make a chef drool with envy. I furiously took notes and wrote a listing. Nate dropped me at the office to pick up my Van and followed me to Viv Appleton's office at Capitol Title.

I furiously typed a listing/lease agreement with an option to purchase. I also wrote a purchase agreement for Nate to buy the house at a pre-determined price. Nate handed Viv a sealed envelope from the seller's lawyer, Maxmillian Snell, who just happens to be my lawyer, too. It contained information on where the Seller, Wanda Poole, was hiding. Viv and Max would be the ONLY people who would know Wanda's address.

When Viv asked Nate for the Earnest Money check, he laid a thick envelope on her desk; Viv took out a stack of one-hundred-dollar bills! I didn't know a jaw could fall that far, that fast; it nearly hit the table. It was all that I could do to keep from laughing out loud.

"Nate, it will take me a couple days to get this signed and recorded. I will call you when you can move into your home." Viv said.

"Thank you so much. We are staying with friends, and my wife, Naomi, is thrilled. Amanda has a Birthday next week, and I am planning a big party!"

He shook both of our hands with a huge smile and left whistling. Viv and I sat back in our chairs. Finally, Viv said, "Hot Damn, Maye, you bring me the most exciting deals! You know it is going to kill me to keep my mouth shut about this, don't you?"

"Little did I know how true those words might become."

"Except for Frank and James, mum's the word! You wouldn't have this deal if there were any doubt of you keeping quiet."

"You know, Maye, if you ever decide to write a book about your experiences in Real Estate and the people you meet, this one has got to be chapter one." Viv laughed.

"Shooting that nasty son of a bitch, Billy Bob Jackson, between the eyes after he whacked Frank beside the head, leaving him lying in a pool of blood, deserves a chapter. He pushed me over the edge when he left poor Lavonne standing in the middle of the room in her panties!

We laughed hugged, and I left to go back to the office. I was sure Ed would love this one, and I couldn't wait to hear his opinion.

When I gave him the file to read, he whistled and said, "Maye, you've got more guts than brains! You DO know that this deal has danger written all over it, don't you?"

"Thank you very much! I finally get a deal I can sink my teeth into, and you throw cold water on it!"

"Sorry, guess I am a little jealous of you getting the juicy stuff. Let me know if you need any help; in the meantime, I will be here plugging away with the same old, same old."

"No problem, you have always been there for me! I appreciate you helping me put the Lake Haverly sale together and getting Frank and George Green home from the Recovery Room. I hope it's because I live, right, and this doesn't bite me in the ass! Seriously, the interest is going higher; we may all have to learn how to put these lease-option deals together, hopefully without the dangerous ex- husbands!" We laughed, never believing for a minute we could be in danger.

A couple days after Viv called to let me know it was signed and recorded, I delivered a lovely bouquet to Nate's house. Nate's beautiful wife, Naomi, ushered me into the kitchen, asking, "Would you like tea or coffee?" Her white-blonde hair, pale blue eyes, and nearly translucent skin starkly contrasted with Nate. When she told me she was a hairdresser and nail technician, I started to hide my hands, then thought better of it and asked for her card. It wouldn't hurt me to be independent of Lavonne. She would be out of the picture when she and John tied the knot; I might have to fend for myself.

Before she hardly exclaimed how grateful they were that I helped them with their home, Nate burst through the door. His arms were full of shopping bags from Toys R Us. He kissed Naomi and asked, "Is Amanda up from her nap yet? I can't wait to see her face when she sees these."

"Nate, you are spoiling Amanda, buying her so many gifts." Naomi admonished him with a smile.

I got up to leave when into the room burst the best of both of them, Miss Amanda! She was a tall four-year-old with sparkling azure eyes surrounded by a light chocolate complexion. I knew the blonde highlights in her curly light brown hair were not from a bottle.

She ran and leaped into Nate's arms, saying, "What did you get me for my Birthday, Daddy?"

"I bought lots of nice things, but you have to wait for the party; darling, Grampa and Gramma are spending a week or two." He said, hugging her as they rubbed noses. Nate thanked me again for helping them. To my surprise and delight, Amanda planted a soft kiss on my cheek, and my heart melted.

Chapter 2 Lake Haverly, here we come!

The small house next to my office posted a "for sale by owner" sign! How dare they put a "FISBO" sign right next to my office! I hot-footed next door and snapped it up before another Office could post their Real Estate for sale sign and make me the laughing stock of the MLS!

Nate dropped by the day after I signed papers on the house with a thank-you card. I opened it and found a gift certificate to Butch's Restaurant in downtown Phoenix. "Nate, thank you so much! Who told you that Butch's is my favorite place to eat?"

"Vivian might have mentioned it. You two did a great job! I am on my way to deliver a card to her; I hope she likes Butch's too."

"She will love it! She and James eat there often; as a matter of fact, the gang hangs out there when we can reserve the Library."

"The Library?"

"Yes, it can be a separate room with bookshelves from table height to the ceilings filled with leather-bound collectible books and replicas of famous works of art. We love the privacy, and Butch Buxton, the owner, personally cooks for us."

"I would love to have my folks meet the people that helped me. They will be in town next week; why don't we set up a time for all of us to have dinner?" Nate said.

"That is a great idea! I would like to meet them, too!"

"What are all these papers?" he asked, seeing them laid all over my desk."

"I am looking at preliminary sketches for plans to add the cottage next door to this building!

"Can I look at them? I was a foreman in my parent's construction company in Chicago until I struck out on my own and came to Arizona," Nate said. He studied the sketches for several minutes. "I can see possibilities for expanding your offices and giving your small apartment upstairs a facelift by adding another bath and bedroom. My

Mom is an architect, and my folks would jump at the chance to spend several months in Phoenix, spoiling Amanda. Will you let them give you an estimate for their company to do the work?"

"Of course, ask your Dad and Mom to come by next week, and we will talk. I plan to keep the homey look my best friend, Lavonne Hall, created. She is a great decorator and will go nuts when she sees the plans and will have sketches for the decorations the minute I give her the go-ahead."

"Hey, have her come over to our house; we need help, too."

"Will do. Lavonne is in Texas but should be back in town soon!

Nate left smiling, and I got back to studying the plans. The little house was separated from my office by a one-car breeze-way. I wanted four offices and an expanded break room, with a full kitchen big enough for meetings.

The phone rang. Frank asked if I wanted company for the weekend. *That chicken still had lips!* I called Butch's Restaurant and ordered a meal delivered, and put my new Office Manager, Mary Ann Noble, in charge of the office. I can't believe I got so lucky to have her walk into my office and apply for the job I hadn't even advertised to fill! Viv heard she was looking for something to keep her busy and sent her to me. It's good to have friends!

Mary Ann was a whizz at organizing and managing her husband's business. She sold her half to his partner when her husband had a fatal heart attack. Working in the office was unimaginable, knowing he would never walk through the door again. She looks 50-something with a slim build and a bawdy sense of humor that surprised the hell out of me!

Shooing me out the door, she said, "Go have fun. I've got everything under control."

Running upstairs to get ready for my weekend with Frank, I showered and dressed. The food arrived, and I put the containers in the oven on low. I placed dishes on the table when I smelled roses and felt strong arms surrounding my body. Lips gently caressed the nape of my neck, sending shivers down my spine.

"Oh, thank you for the fast food delivery. My boyfriend will arrive at any minute."

Turning around in his arms, I said, "Oh, hi, Frank. I thought you were the delivery boy with dinner."

"Maye, did you forget I carry a gun?"

"Did you forget I do too?" I said.

He pulled me close, kissing me passionately, groaning, saying, "Are you starving for food? I have a different hunger."

"We can have dessert before dinner," I said, loosening his tie. We walked to the bedroom in each other's arms, removing clothing. By the time we got to the bed, we had little to stand in our way.

After the loving, we lay in each other's arms until a different hunger possessed us: our stomachs growled loudly. We donned robes, rescued the food from the oven, and devoured the meal. Relaxing and enjoying a couple of bottles of wine, we decided to hide for the weekend.

"You know, Lavonne will be back in town ready to rope me into going to Texas for her wedding. She is going to ask me to be her Mother of the Bride. Didn't she already ask you to walk her down the aisle?"

"Yup, she did! You know they are planning a Western Theme, don't you? There might be ruffles on your dress, but cowboy boots don't have spike heels," he laughed.

"I think I will come dressed as Annie Oakley carrying a shotgun."

Frank laughed, picturing the look on Lavonne's face. "Maye, you know she's got our number, and we will go along with anything she wants!"

"Yeah, I know. No matter how much I protest, Lavonne will bat those big blue eyes, and I will cave." I grabbed both of his hands, bringing them to my chest, saying, "Frank, you've got to protect me!"

"Maye, honey, has anyone ever been able to resist her? She has me dressing up in western gear and walking her down the aisle as her surrogate Father."

"Resistance is futile! Assimilation is inevitable!"

We laughed until an idea popped into my little pea brain. "Frank, Mi, and Josh are out of town, and we should probably check on their property. We can sleep under the stars, skinny dip in the lake, and do a little fishing!"

"I'm game; let's leave right now and wake up listening to birds singing."

"You're on! The fishing and camping gear are in the back of my van. We need food and clothes, and we are good to go."

"You know, Maye, the weather is not exactly conducive to skinny dipping."

"True, but a quick dip in the lake will wake us up, and I can think of several ways to warm up."

"Hold that thought until we get our camp set up; I have a couple of ideas of my own." He said with a silly, lop-sided grin.

We stopped at the closest Walmart, stocked the cooler with enough food for a weekend, and were on the road in an hour.

The drive to Punkin Center was beautiful, with the fall colors and the newly paved road. We eagerly opened the gate, cresting the hill overlooking Lake Haverly. The view always takes our breath away, and we were excited to see the Eagle family in the tall fir tree on the lake's far shore.

The persistent drought condition of Arizona does not affect Lake Haverly, which is maintained by an artesian well. It makes a great story, but it is not a proven fact; people believe Lake Haverly was part of the Pacific Ocean thousands of years ago. There are rumors of pre-historic species of fish in its depth.

We decided to visit with the other two residents, Mrs. Soderman and Fred Potts, tomorrow. Frank was mentally tasting Mrs. Soderman's fresh bread; my taste buds were itching for her cookies, and Fred would load us up with fruits and veggies. I checked out Mi and Josh's house while Frank unpacked our equipment and set up camp. He lit the fire in the Coleman, adding a couple potatoes.

We were just finishing our steaks when we saw a boat pulling up to the wharf. The third property owner, James Crandall and Viv Appleton, stepped out. James tested Ed's and my patience and sales abilities when Mi and Josh bought his property. James was devastated to learn one of his long-lost sons was the body in Lake Haverly. He and his other son, John Kinney, a veterinarian from Texas, never opened the paternity report. They looked so much alike; we were sure they were Father and son. John and my BBF Lavonne Hall fell in love at first sight, and I am still coming to terms with her living in Texas!

They hugged us, saying, "We were just coming over to check the house, but I guess you already did that."

Frank lit the propane fireplace, and we got comfy around the fire, catching up on our lives and enjoying the beer they thoughtfully brought. The conversation turned to the wedding. James asked, "Have you got your marching orders from Lavonne of what you will wear yet?"

"Oh, yes, I have my Annie Oakley outfit with the shotgun packed, and Frank had his horse shipped down to Texas. You know the one, he will sling Lavonne over the saddle and ride up the aisle wearing his western Sheriff's outfit, shooting his six guns. It will be spectacular!"

The look on their faces was priceless until Frank and I started laughing our asses off.

"Come in, tell us the truth; what is she making you wear?" Viv asked.

"I don't have the foggiest! I haven't heard a word from the little vixen! Lavonne better not try to put me in spike heels again; the last time, I fell on my ass! I am a low-heel kinda gal with no frills! I will put my foot down!"

They all looked at me with that 'Yeah right' look, and I said, "What? You don't think I can put my foot down?"

"Oh yeah, you will put it down, alright! Right in the shoe she picks for you, and it will barely show under the dress you will wear," Viv said, giggling, and then everyone downright snorted.

"That's not very nice! Just for that, we are all going skinny dipping. Come on, you guys; shuck those clothes!" I got up and started doing a striptease as I removed my top. Frank got into the swing of it, wiggling his hips as he yanked his t-shirt over his head. We were sure Viv and James would chicken out, but not so!

James hollered, "The last one in is a chicken!" as he removed the last of his clothes, sprinting towards the lake.

We all dove into the icy water, coming up screaming like banshees and running the 4-minute mile to our fire and into our clothes. Frank turned up the propane fireplace to warm us up. We huddled until we stopped shivering, laughing like idiots!

Viv asked, "Has Nate mentioned about all of us getting together for Dinner at Butches. Maye, I hardly ever get gifts from clients."

"It was nice of him to do that, but you did a bang-up job putting that deal together; we may have to do more of them if the interest rate goes any higher."

"Good thing, Girl, we have a leg up on the competition." She said, high-fiving me.

"Max was helpful with the wording to nail it together."

"He has been a valuable asset to me."

James said, "Well, guys, think we will call it a night."

After hugs all around, they rowed for James's house across the lake.

Frank put his arms around me and whispered, "I thought they would never leave."

"Yeah, I enjoyed the swim, but we should wait until spring for another."

We stripped and crawled into our two-person sleeping bag on the blow-up mattress. We were enjoying our bodies touching each other when Frank whispered, "Maye, I can't imagine my life without you. You know I love you, don't you? What do you think about making this permanent?

Oh! Oh! He was entering dangerous territory!

"I love you, too, Frank. What do you mean by making it permanent?"

"We could get married."

"Frank, we both love our time together and our alone time. Do you think we can still live together full-time and have our alone time, too?"

"I know we both get involved in our careers and are apart for days at a time, and I love our reunions."

"I do, too, but we aren't getting caught up in John and Lavonne's wedding, are we?"

"Maybe a little, but we could try it for a few weeks and see how we feel?"

"You mean like a trial marriage? Do we stay at my apartment or move into your Condo?"

"Let's decide in the morning; I have some pressing demands I would like to address right now."

Pulling me close, I felt his demands, so we both concentrated on each other to a satisfactory conclusion.

In the morning, we decided Frank would move more clothes into my house in addition to the fresh uniform he keeps in my closet. We agreed not to share our trial marriage.

Frank had no sooner got his things put away when his cell rang. Our "honeymoon" was short-lived.

"Maye, a woman was murdered in her home close to your option house on Columbine Ave. From what the officer told me, it is messy, so don't wait up. He kissed me and left. Frank did not return that night or the next morning!

Returning from a listing appointment, I noticed a big red truck with Texas plates parked in front of my office. Lavonne accosted me with a hug the minute I walked into the break room.

"Maye, where have you been? I've been waiting for hours."

"Lavonne, you do know that I work for a living, don't you?" I said as I tried to extricate myself from her arms to put my papers down. *"Did she grow longer arms in two weeks?"*

"I need to talk to you and Frank about the wedding."

"Frank is pleased as punch you asked him to walk you down the aisle.

"Maye, you and Frank are dear to me, like the parents I never had." She said, with tears already forming in those lovely blue eyes. *"Man, I am so screwed!"*

Lavonne barely comes to my shoulders, and I am vertically challenged! Her head, with her beautiful curly salt and pepper hair, was resting on my shoulder. My arms automatically wrapped around her; she looked up at me and said. "Maye, I've got a big favor to ask you."

"Lavonne, you know there isn't anything in this world I wouldn't do for you except for spike heels, ruffles, and bows."

"I promise, no spike heels or bows, but there might be a few ruffles!" Giving me that teary smile that melts my heart.

"A few? If that means one or two, you got it. What do you need?"

"I would love for you to be my Mother of the Bride."

"Lavonne, I will be honored." Now, we both had free-flowing tears. Her Grandmother raised her since she was a baby after her parents died. The unbending rules pushed Lavonne into eloping with her husband. He was a big man, and gentle was not in his strong suit! She is tiny, and the first time they had sex, he nearly killed her; after being rushed to the ER, she cannot have children.

Gramma left Lavonne a sizable estate, and during their bitter divorce, the ex got most of it. Lavonne didn't give a damn about the money! She was thrilled when I told her I planned to pull up stakes and move to Arizona! She hitched her wagon behind mine in the wagon train, and off we went.

"Now, Maye, you and Frank are going to be fitted for your outfits. Since John is a Texan, I am planning to create a real Texas-style wedding! What do you think?" She said, her eyes as big as saucers, with a yearning expression waiting for my enthusiastic response.

I wouldn't rain on her parade unless she started talking about ruffles and bows. "I think a Western theme will be fun and more comfortable than formal wedding attire. Are you getting married here in Arizona, or are we all going to Texas?"

"I'm not sure. John has a brother and a sister with kids in Texas, but they are anxious to visit James. It would be easier, and we wouldn't take you and Frank away from your work, and your agents will want to come too, won't they?"

"Yes, of course, they will! All our friends would love to be part of your wedding."

"You are right; I am sure John will agree that having it here will be better."

John will agree to anything she wants, and she knows it, too.

"All I have to do is find the perfect venue for the ceremony and reception."

"Aren't you getting a little ahead of yourself? Shouldn't you set the date?"

"Oh, it will be in June. That way, I will have all winter to plan my perfect wedding." She said, hugging herself, looking ecstatic.

"Good, can you work two jobs in between your wedding planning? I bought that little house next door and am having it connected to this building. I want to make offices for the agents and a big break/conference room. My apartment will be enlarged, with two bedrooms and two baths. Nate Harris, the young man who bought the house on Columbine Ave in that new subdivision in North West Peoria, wants your help to re-decorate. When his parents get here, they will give me an estimate for the construction. I was hoping you would have time to decorate the offices and the new break room, of course, I will understand if you are not too busy.

"Maye West! You know I wouldn't let anyone else touch your office! I should look at the plans to be sure you thought of everything." She said with an impish grin.

I hugged her again and said, "It's good to have you home, even if you are rushing back to Texas again."

"You won't get rid of me that easy! Fall is John's busiest time, and I will stay here, going to Texas periodically to be with him."

After pouring over the sketches for several minutes, Lavonne pronounced them perfect. She would have sketches for decorating in a couple of days. Now that she had what she wanted, she flitted out the door. I was left wondering what kind of a mess Frank was dealing with.

Chapter 3 The Murder Scene and spilled beans

I walked outside for a breath of fresh air. You never get used to the sight and smell of death at crime scenes; nothing erases the odor, and the picture becomes permanently etched behind your eyes.

I whipped Vicks Vapor Rub under my nose, wishing it would kill the smell, but I knew it would only mask it enough to keep my stomach down. As the first responder, my gloves, booties, and cover-all kept me from contaminating the crime scene. My training helped separate the grisly reality from the business of searching for clues. The 'why' may not become evident for months or years.

The living room of this lovely suburban home was splattered with blood from the floor, reaching halfway to the vaulted ceiling. Decorating the living room was a mostly nude body in an unnatural position, showing signs of a brutal beating. Bloody, tattered pieces of clothes were strewn over much of the surrounding area; cigarette burns on her arms and legs looked like ugly, nonsensical tattoos. The cause of death would have to wait for the report from the Coroner, George Green.

As I looked at the crime scene, I thought, "*She was one tough woman! She was surprised but not unprepared, and she put up a hell of a fight! There is too much blood! It can't be all hers! Whoever she shot was carried out! The pistol jammed in that particular orifice tells me those sons-of-bitchs got even with her for having the nerve to shoot one or hopefully two of them. I can't help hoping she got more than one of the bastards, and it was fatal!*"

I briefed my officers about the scene. "Officer Brannen, I want pictures of every square inch of that house! Don't assume it isn't important! Someone tortured that poor woman and made a mess searching for something."

"Yes, sir. I have my crime kit in the car. Do you want any samples, or should I wait for CSI?" Officer Brannen asked.

"Just take pictures: tons of pictures! Let the CSI do their thing." She smiled as I passed the Vicks Vapor Rub bottle to her, slipping it into her pocket.

"Shirl, you will take the lead. Direct the officers waiting for orders to canvas the neighborhood. I want to know what anyone saw or heard tonight. Have all the reports and pictures on my desk by 10:00 a.m. tomorrow." I said as I stripped the protective clothing and booties off.

"Yes, sir," He said, looking at his watch. He immediately walked briskly to the group of officers waiting for orders. I smiled when I heard him saying, "Everyone, gather around. We will be canvassing the immediate neighborhood, but I need two officers to canvass the surrounding area." Shirl spread a map of the subdivision on the hood of a squad car. He gave the officers their assignments. "Remember, we want information from the residents! Do not give ANY information! If and when the Press shows up, anyone only says No Comment! Got it? There had better not be any leaks!"

I couldn't help but smile at the chorus of, "Yes, Sir!" Now that everyone had their orders and scattered to carry them out, I relaxed. The second my head touched the back of the seat, exhaustion took over, and I passed out.

My head nearly hit the cab roof when Shirl knocked on my window. Rolling it down, I asked him how the canvassing was going? "Boss, it is after midnight; we have canvassed the entire neighborhood. We will finish the rest of the subdivision tomorrow morning. I sent the guys home with instructions to have their notes on my desk at 8:00 a.m. and will have my report in your hands before 10:00 a.m. I'd like to head home for a few hours shut-eye unless you need anything else from me tonight?"

"No, did anyone hear or see anything?"

"I wish! It is amazing how people suddenly become deaf and blind when you ask them about a murder next door.

"Go home and get some sleep; I am planning on doing the same thing." I shook myself awake enough to drive to Maye's. I wondered how I was going to keep from spilling the beans to her. She would be up waiting to hear about it because of how close it was to her option house on Columbine.

I was not surprised to see lights on upstairs when I parked in the back of Maye's office. Auto-pilot took over: locking the car, climbing the stairs, putting the key in the lock, and quietly opening the door. I didn't need to be quiet; Maye stood inside, her arms folded across her chest. Patiently waiting for me to spill those beans that I had no intention of spilling.

I guess the look on my face told her the story of my day and evening. She said nothing, pulling me into her arms and holding me for several minutes. God, she smelled good! I could feel myself starting to sag, and she did, too!

"Come with me, Mister!" She put her arm around my waist and walked me through her apartment out to the back, where she had the hot tub bubbling in minutes. I stood there like a zombie while she unbuttoned my shirt and slipped off my pants, shoes, and socks. I would have fallen into the hot tub head first, like a little kid, if she hadn't helped me. I leaned back against the Jets and, for the first time in hours, thought only of Maye as she let her robe drop to the floor and slipped in beside me. Our wet bodies felt good and molded together, absorbing the relaxing pulse of the jets.

"Maye," I started to say, but she shushed me by kissing me. I was so exhausted; all I could do was kiss back half-heartedly. She helped me dry off and slipped the robe around me, walking me to the bed. I saw the bed already turned down, and I would have fallen if Maye hadn't helped me to bed. The sleep of the dead claimed me until morning.

I woke early, enjoying having Frank's body next to mine, knowing he would head to the office as soon as his eyes opened. I slipped out, leaving him sleeping, returning in a few minutes.

His eyes opened when he smelled the freshly brewed coffee. Sipping the steaming brew, he held up his hand, saying, "Maye, I know you want information about the murder, but not this morning, please. I promise I will tell you everything tonight after all the reports arrive."

"But, Frank, I am worried about Nate and his family. You know if the sale and this murder are connected, we will need to protect everyone!"

"Hon, I promise if there is ANY connection, I will make sure they are protected, but you are my main concern." His eyes showed the worry for my safety that mine must show for him and my clients.

"Thanks," I said, leaning in, kissing him, and nuzzling his neck. He pulled back a little, saying. "Now, Maye, you stop that! You will not get me to tell you the details by getting me all hot and bothered." He had that silly grin on his face I love, and I decided to see how hot and bothered he would get. I snuggled close with my arms around him, slinging my leg over his body and sliding onto his lap. Smothering him with kisses, I whispered in his ear, "How hot and bothered do I need to make you?"

Groaning, he said, "Not much more, but please, not now." I reluctantly let him get dressed, and over coffee and breakfast, he did spill some of the beans. I didn't let on that his edited description of the crime scene horrified me. Later, when my imagination ran wild, I would be plagued with nightmares for months. He admonished me to keep the crime scene description to myself. I crossed my fingers behind my back as I vowed to say nothing.

After showering, I headed downstairs to see my best friend, Fast Eddie! I sauntered into his office with two cups of coffee and blueberry muffins on a tray. I didn't fool him for a second! Looking up smiling, he said, "Good Morning, Maye, what's up?"

"What makes you think anything is up?"

"Maye, when was the last time you came visiting with muffins and coffee? Come on, spill it. Frank told you all about the crime scene, and you need to talk. You brought the right incentive; you've got my attention." He said, taking a big bite of his muffin.

He listened intently to the details of the crime scene; he already knew the details of Nate's deal. He sat thinking for a couple of minutes. He said, "Maye, we don't have enough information to form a solid conclusion, but I think Frank is right to take a 'wait and see' attitude. He promised if your clients were in danger, he would protect them, didn't he?"

"Yes, he did, but..."

"Maye, let him do his job! He said, giving me "the look," you know, the one that says 'don't do it,' but knowing whether I would heed his advice was iffy.

"Thanks, Ed, you are always a voice of reason. I am worried that Wanda's ex-husband, Clarence, will include us in his revenge plans!

"Maye, maybe you should save the worrying until you know whether this murder had anything to do with your deal? Didn't you tell me the ex-husband is in prison and will be for several years?"

"Right, Frank should check on it."

"Maye, I will wager Frank already checked. This murder may not be connected to your clients at all if Clarence is still in prison.

"You're right. I'll ask Frank tonight when he gets home."

"When he gets home?" Ed's eyebrows shot up to his hairline, which is getting further north every year. "Is there something you want to share with the class?"

He had that knowing look on his face. Dammit, I've got to be more careful;

Ed is way too smart for his britches. I knew if he found out about our arrangement, I could count on him to keep my secret, but Frank and I agreed to keep it on the down low. We wanted time to get used to the idea and make sure it would work before sharing it with everyone.

That marriage thing is a big step, and neither Frank nor I had ever given it much thought. God, if Lavonne found out, she would have us marching down the aisle before the year was out.

"I had to find a way to detour Ed's mind before he started asking questions, and I spilled my guts!"

"Frank was planning on spending the night. Why are you suddenly interested in my sex life? I don't question you about yours and Kay's."

I have rarely seen Ed blush until now, and he dropped the subject.

Chapter 4 "Outed" and meeting Nate's parents

Mary Ann interrupted me, preparing a listing presentation, "Maye, Nate Harris is here with his parents; shall I send them in?"

"No, I'll come out and greet them." I hurried to the front office.

"Hello, Maye. I want to introduce you to my parents, Alfred and Michelle Harris." Nate proudly offered. We shook hands, "It is nice to meet you; let's go into my office where we can sit comfortably. Would you like coffee or tea and muffins?"

"Thanks, coffee would be nice. We had breakfast," Michelle answered.

I couldn't help observing Nate and his parents' contrast as we walked to my office. Where Nate was tall and slim, his parents barely reached his shoulder. Michelle's coloring matched Nate's; her short afro framed her beautiful face with nary a wrinkle. Alfred looked like a short version of an older Nate with a little more meat on his frame. Alfred wore a business suit and tie, and I didn't need Lavonne to tell me it was custom. The simplicity and the cut of Michelle's dress and the fabric whispered designer, and she draped an amazing black fur coat on the back of her chair.

"Cream or sugar in your coffee?"

"Thanks, we like it black," Michelle answered for all.

Nate followed me to the break room and carried the tray with a carafe and four cups back to my office; he poured the coffee.

"Nate tells me you own a construction company in Chicago."

"Yes, we do. My friends call me Al. Mich and I have worked together for over 30 years and have had the honor to build many fine homes."

"Nate was telling us about your sketches," Al said.

"I often wished for two bedrooms and another bath, but I didn't want to give up my exercise area. After coffee, we can look at them together, and you can tell me if that is possible."

"You and Mich can work out the details; she is my architect; I build whatever she dreams up," Al said proudly, glancing at Mich.

"We both will, Dad," Nate said.

"Maye, I love the weather here in Phoenix! I understand it is only an hour or two to ski country and beaches. Maybe I can convince Al to leave the cold snow country to come here and enjoy these mild winters."

"It's true, it rarely snows in the Phoenix, but we can fry an egg on the sidewalk in the summer, and when the temperature climbs to 120 degrees, most people head for the hills. I tell my clients we live in paradise in the winter and the other place in the summer."

Mich laughed. "Your homes and business are air-conditioned, aren't they?"

"Yes, they are; I love it here in the high desert. It is beautiful, and I wouldn't want to live anywhere else. I don't miss the changing seasons; I had my fill of that being from Maine. The business climate changes from hour to hour; it is nice to have one constant in my life. I am impressed with your portfolio, and if we agree on the changes to the plans, you can draw them for me if you want the job."

"Speaking of impressive, helping Nate buy that house was short of a miracle. We will be forever grateful for your help."

"After meeting Amanda, I am happy he let me help him; she stole my heart."

"She stole ours, too, the minute we saw her. This project will give us an excuse to spend time with her," Mich said, looking at Al. I have time this week to work on the plans. As you know, the guys have planned a big Birthday Party for Miss Amanda. She is turning five. I will work on the changes while the guys are busy. We would love for you to stop by for cake and ice cream."

"Thank-you. I would love that!"

"Don't worry about a gift; Miss Amanda needs no more gifts." She said, looking at Nate: he smiled back at her.

"My best friend, Lavonne Hall, will know just what to get; she decorated my office."

"I love the homey yet the business look she achieved. I may ask Lavonne to come to Chicago and re-decorate our offices."

"She would love to do that; right now, her big project is planning her June wedding here in Arizona."

"I would love to meet her; why don't you bring her with you to the party."

"She will love that; she adores children."

Our meeting broke up, and the Harrises went on their way.

The morning of Amanda's birthday party dawned warm and dry, with a slight breeze prompting Nate and Naomi to set the kids' table under a big umbrella next to the patio. At the same time, the adults sat in the shade with fans and drinks.

Lavonne selected the perfect gift, an American Girl doll dressed in a party dress. It brought squeals of delight from Amanda and smiles of approval from her parents and grandparents. The Harrises promised Lavonne two more jobs in Chicago. Mich had finished working on the additions to my plan, and Al and Nate were ready to start construction when the deal was recorded.

We were having a great time watching Amanda and her friends running, playing, and screaming with delight at each new thing Al and Nate arranged: a pony for the kids to ride and a blow-up slide.

I was lost in the fantasy world of kids squealing with delight and enjoying the adult refreshments. I smiled when I looked up and saw Frank standing on the sidelines. It took me several minutes to realize he had not been invited.

"Folks, I am sorry to interrupt your party, but I would like to take Maye away for a few minutes; would you please excuse us?" Frank took my arm and led me to his cruiser.

Still in a party mood, sitting in the front seat next to Frank, I started telling him all about the stuff Nate and Al had planned. He interrupted me, "Maye, I'm sorry, but I need your attention; please drink some coffee."

Seeing the serious look on his face, I downed half the coffee and started coming out of the Happy Birthday fog. I realized Frank would not ask me to leave the party unless necessary.

"Frank, what is wrong?" Scared to death to hear the answer but anxious to learn what was this important!

"Maye, we discovered another body this morning, and we are pretty sure this one is connected to your option sale."

"Who was it?" My mind was racing through a list of everyone with a connection.

"We don't know for sure."

"What? What do you mean, you don't know?"

"Maye, it was a male, and he was found in Max's office. It was a mess; someone was looking for something!

"Oh my God, was it Max? It can't be Max!"

"We don't know; we are waiting for identification from the Coroner."

"Frank, take me to the Coroner's office right now. I can tell you if it is Max!"

"Maye, that is not a good idea; the condition of the body will make it difficult for the Coroner to make an identification. I promise you, once the body is identified if you still want to go, I will take you to the morgue."

"Max is my friend Frank; if this is related to my Option house, we must warn everyone involved with this sale."

"Maye, let's be sure this was not about one of his cases. CSI is working the scene right now, but I wanted to tell you before you heard it on the news. Max's files will determine if any of their clients had a reason to do him harm. We know the other victim interacted with Wanda's ex-husband several times. She called the police when Clarence came home drunk and abused Wanda."

"How soon will the identification be done?"

"Hopefully, tomorrow. I will be working long hours for several days. Please don't tell anyone about this. A deputy will cruise the neighborhood, and the local police will do the same for everyone involved. Maye, will you be okay going back to the party?" He asked, putting his arms around me.

"I am stronger than the average bear; besides, I pack; I never leave home without Miranda. I must go back! If I don't, they will know something is wrong! Right now, I need to stay in your arms if you don't mind."

"It will be my pleasure as long as you want."

We hugged for several minutes; I kissed Frank more passionately than I intended. "Keep that up, and we might be in trouble when the patrol car arrives any minute to take over for me." He said but didn't move out of my arms. After a few minutes, I downed the last coffee, took a deep breath, eased out of his arms, and opened the door.

"Hon, I may be late tonight. Get some sleep; tomorrow will be a busy day for you when the reporters get the news."

"Hi Ho, Hi Ho, it's back to the party. I must go." I sang as I pasted a happy smile on my face.

No one but Lavonne guessed anything was wrong; later, she would insist on an edited version.

Frank finally came home in the wee hours; the minute his head hit the pillow, he was out like a light. I let him sleep later than usual, and the minute he got a sip of coffee, I blurted out, "Frank, I need to know what's going on."

With a sigh, he said, "Maye, we know the neighbor lady came in contact with Clarence. Max may have known where Wanda is hiding, and we think that is the connection between the two murders. There was an attempted jailbreak last night at Florence Prison. They are checking every inmate, and we will know who or if anyone successfully escaped later this morning." Before I could ask more questions, he held up his hand and said. "Maye, I promise I will tell you everything as soon as possible."

"Frank, what if Clarence escaped? And he killed Max! OMG, all I did was help a nice kid get a home for his family! I'm not sure I can face losing Max or any of our friends getting hurt!" I said, trying without success to keep the waterworks from sliding down my face.

Frank took my hands in his and said, "I promise I will call the minute I have any information. Officers are re-canvassing the neighborhood around your option house. Maye, you know if there is the slightest chance that you or any of our friends are in danger, I will take steps to protect everyone. You have no blame for someone else doing harm."

"I know, but I will worry until they are safe." I dried my tears, and Frank kissed me goodbye and held me in his arms a little longer, saying, "You know, I could get used to waking up next to you every morning. I am liking the idea of cuddling with you until I fall asleep at night and not having to drive home."

"Frank, it's only been a week! Let's give it a little more time before we completely change our lives. Okay?"

"You know, when they start construction, we may be "outed" whether we want to be or not, don't you?"

"Why don't we cross that bridge when we come to it?"

Kissing me again, Frank left by the back door, and I went down to my office.

"Good morning, Maye. The phone has been ringing off the hook, mostly newspapers wanting to know if we had any comment about the murder last night. We don't, do we?" Mary Ann asked.

"That's right!"

"Good, because I told them all, no comment!"

"Thanks, Mary Ann. Sorry, I am late. I overslept; I guess I partied too much at the birthday yesterday. How did the reporters get information so fast?"

"I don't know, but did Frank tell you why they are calling? I saw him leave." Mary Anne smiled, eyebrow raised a little. I knew she knew everything that went on in my office, but until now, I was unaware of how much Mary Anne knew about my private life.

Ignoring her question, I said, "Mary Anne, when Mrs. Harris gets here, please show her right in; she will have the finished plans for our offices. She is the only one I need to see; buzz me before you let anyone else in. Thanks."

"Okay," She left, shutting my door.

I started remembering the things Max had done for me. Smart Realtors write transactions so that a ten-year-old can understand them. However, when you delve into commercial properties, a lawyer can be your best friend. Max has drafted several complicated business transactions. I blurted out loud, "I am going to miss that, old Son-a-Bitch!"

Mary Anne, walking back from the break room, heard me and opened the door, peeking in, asked, "Maye, is everything alright? Can I do anything?"

"Come in and sit down; I need to bring you up to date on what is happening. Maxmillion Snell is a good friend and has been my attorney for many years; he may have been murdered last night. He is one of the few people we think knew where Wanda Poole was living. Her ex-husband vowed to kill her and anyone helping her, and that may include many of my friends." I said, hoping she wouldn't bolt for the door!

"Maye, don't worry about me; I am used to people not being happy with the boss. I don't advertise it, but I have a concealed permit, and I keep a loaded gun in my purse."

I couldn't help releasing a breath as I said, "Good, that makes me feel better. You know I carry, and if you read the news last year, you know that I am not afraid to shoot!"

"Yes, your shoot-out last year gave me a good laugh. I've got to know, was your intention to hit the guy right between the eyes?"

"Yes, it was!"

"Maye, I am sure glad we are friends; I would not want you for an enemy."

"Mary Anne, you are not in any danger from me. I don't know how I ever got along without you."

Most of the morning, I sat in my office alone, periodically breaking down and letting the tears flow, then pulling myself together. I tried to concentrate on work, but everything kept flying out of my head except the enormity of Max's death. I heard a gentle knock about noontime and could smell the delicious aroma of fresh burgers and fries. Instantly, my stomach started growling as Frank came through the door, carrying a big bag from Wendy's.

"Man, am I glad to see you! I forgot to eat anything this morning. How many burgers did you bring?"

"Two, but there are fries and two large chocolate Frostys."

"You are a lifesaver, thank you!" Digging into the bag, handing him one, and unwarping the other, I already had a big bite in my mouth before he got his unwrapped.

"Maye, I have some news that may cheer you up a little," he said through a Mouth full of burger. "Max was out of town last weekend, so he was not the person who was killed!"

I let out a breath and felt my body relax until I realized it was someone else from Max's office. He would be devastated!

"I am relieved it wasn't Max, but he is going to be pissed! Do you know who?"

"No, not yet; I am expecting the coroner's report this afternoon. There have been no leaks to the Press yet! That is good news; I don't want to deal with another wrong identification!."

"I don't know, rescuing you and George from the Recovery Room was the highlight of Fast Eddie's and my evening last year." I couldn't help ribbing him about him and George getting drunk after identifying the body in Lake Haverly as James Crandall. It wasn't Frank and George's finest hour when James showed up at his memorial service mad as hell.

We finished our lunch, setting back; Frank brought up the subject of Nate Harris.

"Maye, what exactly do we know about Nate? He seems like a nice young man, but where did he get $30,000.00 for a down payment? All we know for sure is he worked as a handyman and hairstylist?"

"His parents may have helped him with the money. You know, Frank, I am not under any obligation to find out where clients get their money to purchase houses."

"I know, but aren't you a little curious about how he maintains his lifestyle?"

"Yes, a little, but Naomi must make a good living from her shop, and he isn't quite as young as he looks. He could have been saving for years for this purchase."

"Yes, that may be true, but I am curious about how he found out about Wanda wanting to sell her house? Nate had to know Wanda and may have known Clarence. Nate could be in danger whether he knows or doesn't know where she is hiding. He either made a deal with Wanda before she left town or was contacted by her. I pulled Clarence's rap sheet, and that guy is one badass! He was a suspect in several assault cases against women. Most women did not file, and the ones re-canted when threatened. If I didn't know better, I would think he is our perpetrator in both crimes." Frank said, running his hand through his hair.

"Do you think there is a connection between Nate and Clarence?

"I don't know for sure, but it gives me pause. By the way, Clarence didn't break out of prison. I talked to the warden, and he must have someone outside doing his bidding."

"I feel better knowing he is behind bars, but knowing he has people on the outside to carry out his plans is not good."

"We are looking into former cellmates and anyone close to him, in or out of prison. If we find anything, I will keep you informed."

"I am looking forward to the dinner party on Saturday night. It will be good to be with friends."

"I can think of a way to relax before the party."

"I like the sound of that; how about tonight?"

"You've got a deal. We could stay at my Condo; there is a pool and a hot tub!"

"Yeah, but we have to wear swimsuits, and I'm not sure where I put mine."

"I'm not sure where mine is either." He said as he left.

I always wondered how he could leave his work at the office and be his affable self when we were together. Now, living with him, I know he can't always. I could see the toll it takes on him. Our time together helps us face the outside world; we shed our cloaks of strength and heal each other.

Minutes after Frank left, Mich and Al strolled in with the plans for the addition to my building. We went to the break room to lay the several layers on the table. Mich had extended my apartment to two bedrooms and two baths and still had room to install the hot tub for me, a weight bench, and a treadmill for Frank, with the suggestion of a sauna. When she showed me the upgraded kitchen, I didn't have the heart to tell her I couldn't boil water without it burning. Lavonne will laugh and squeal on me when she sees the plans. I missed the "Susie Homemaker" gene. The only thing I do well is to make reservations.

I oohed and ahhed over the renovations, and when I asked how long it would take for it to be move-in ready, they both looked at each other and smiled. Finally, Mich said, "We estimate it will be move-in ready before Christmas. There will be several weeks when your apartment will be open to prying eyes. Frank has a condo, so you will have a place to stay."

The look on my face must have given it away because they continued to look at me wide-eyed, with slight smiles on their faces.

"My God, don't I have any secrets? Does everyone know my business?" I sputtered, hiding my red face in my hands.

"Maye, I am sorry if we weren't supposed to know, but the office is quietly buzzing; they think it is cute and decided to keep quiet until you announced something. Lavonne was so excited, she was almost bursting to tell someone." Mich said.

"Frank and I wanted a trial of a few weeks of living together. What a disaster! Doesn't she have enough to do planning her own wedding? I've got to nip this in the bud! Can I trust you to keep this under your hat?"

They were both smiling, not as big as before. "Maye, no one knows about your private life; however, the noise and lack of privacy will make a move necessary. We will work as fast as we can and inconvenience you as little as possible."

"I am sorry if it felt like I was snapping at you; this renovation and the wedding are stressing me more than I expected," I said, hoping to smooth their ruffled feathers.

"No worries, Maye, we understand, but it is sweet how much your friends love and respect you. If you approve of our suggestions, we can start work as soon as the papers are signed. The building permits are ready to submit. We plan to keep all the vintage woodwork, cupboards, and doors, save as much of the ceramic tile as possible, and will try to find more to match."

"Thank you for your attention to detail; I am looking forward to seeing it finished.

After they left, I leaned back in my chair and thought about how I would tell Frank that we had been "outed."

Chapter 5 Lavonne, the FBI, Max, and Viv

My office became my sanctuary when I had a problem I needed to solve. I locked the door and paced the room, imagining solutions to the wagging tongue of my BBF Lavonne! I love her to pieces, but she can be a pain in my ass! I could buy a swimsuit and stay at Frank's Condo for several weeks, but we would definitely be outed. I needed a place to sleep during the renovation, preferably with Frank!

Looking around my office, I gobsmacked myself on the forehead, realizing the solution was staring me right in the face! I have a couch and a bath accessible from my office and the hall. I'd just have to remember to lock the adjoining door; it wouldn't be good to have my agents or clients catch me in the buff.

Frank could stay in his Condo, which might quell the wagging tongues. I hated that idea. I was getting used to cuddling with him every night and waking up next to him in the morning.

A knock on the door startled me from my reverie; in walked, or I should say exploded, Lavonne! She was juggling a stack of books that looked like they weighed more than her tiny body. I rushed to take them from her before they dropped.

"Thanks, Maye; these books have tons of ideas for planning my perfect Western Wedding!"

"Is it going to be formal western or casual western? Remember, I said no spike heels and ruffles! As the Mother of the Bride, I get a say in the wearing apparel, don't I?"

"Yes, of course, I have it mostly planned, except for a few touches."

"Such as what?" I half wanted to know and was half scared to death.

"I had my heart set on an authentic Western wedding! I discovered poor families had no-frills, simple weddings, and you know I am not a plain Jane type of gal." She smiled up at me, showing her adorable dimples.

Continuing, she said, "You and Frank lean toward simple, but my John wants me to have the wedding of my dreams! I think I have come up with the perfect compromise. "

The dreamy look on her face was scaring me to death! I couldn't stand it any longer and blurted out, "For heavens sakes, tell me what you have in mind for Frank and me to wear. I will go along with a big fancy wedding as long as...

At that point, Lavonne interrupted me, saying, "Maye, sweetie, I promise there will be no spike heels or ruffles!" She burst out laughing, seeing the relief on my face, throwing her tiny arms around me and giving me a big hug.

"Well, dig into your bag of tricks and show me some sketches; you do have sketches, don't you?" I begged.

"I sort of scratched some ideas in my wedding notebook, but they aren't ready to show yet." She said with an innocent look on her devious little face. With an impish look, she added, "How do you feel about Denim?"

"If you don't have any information or sketches to show me, be gone!" I said, waving my arms and scooting her toward the door!

"I am about to make reservations for a dinner party on Saturday night at Butch's, and by the way, you are coming, aren't you?"

"Who else is coming?"

"Never mind! Just come, and you will see, and by the way, we will be in the Library. Did you bring those books with you today to force me to look through all of them? Or are they just to scare me to death?"

"No, they are for my eyes only." She said smugly, picking them up and stacking them in her arms. If I hadn't seen it with my own eyes, I wouldn't believe she could carry them all; she is tiny but wiry.

"Well, remove yourself from my inner sanctum so I can get some work done."

She huffed out of my office. Turning, she blew me a kiss with the sweetest smile on her face and disappeared.

I placed a call, and Butch answered himself, "Butches Restaurant, How may I help you?"

"Butch, is business so bad that you have to answer the phone yourself?" I laughed.

"Maye darling, how wonderful to hear from you, it's been ages! We are busy, and my manager took a few days off. Am I going to be seeing your beautiful face soon?"

"I just can't stay away from you, Butch, you devil! Tell me the Library is available this Saturday night, pretty please!"

"For you, M'Lady, I will move heaven and earth! Are you still hitched up with that tall drink of water, Fred?"

"Butch, you know very well, his name is Frank. And try to remember we both carry guns, darling."

"I will be on my best behavior just for you, Sweet Thing. How many people will you be bringing?"

Let me see; there will be Frank, Lavonne, Al and Mich Harris, Nate and Naomi Harris, for sure, and maybe two or three more couples."

"No problem. The Library will accommodate a party of up to 30. We can close the partition for a small party and make it intimate. I presume you want your usual party dinner. That will be on the 17th of October, right?"

"Yes, perfect! If there are any changes, I will call. You will make sure there will be plenty of chilled champagne?"

"Of course. Don't I always make it perfect? By the way, it has been ages since you have come in for one of your 'Champagne Lunches!' I will save my most intimate booth for you. I miss gazing into those mesmerizing green eyes! I still stock half bottles of champagne, just for you. I will personally make your open-face Crab and Cheese on our fresh baked English muffin."

"Oooh! You know how to tempt a girl, and it has been ages. Thanks, Butch; I will check with Frank to see how soon we can make it," I said as I hung up. Butch is such a cool guy; we have been friends for more years than either of us wants to admit, and he is so good for my ego.

If my life wasn't complicated enough, another speed bump was approaching via the phone call I was about to receive. It sent me into hypervigilance; it isn't every day that a Realtor meets with an FBI agent!

Mary Anne buzzed me, saying, "Maye, you have a phone call from Agent Ward Stone of the FBI! Do you need a minute before I put it through?"

"No problem put him through," I said, more confident than I felt.

"Ms. West, I am liaising with the Phoenix Police Department and the Sheriff's Office. Would a meeting this morning be convenient?"

"Certainly, Mr. Stone, would 10:00 at my office work for you?"

"Thank you; it would. " Mr. Stone immediately hung up.

Mary Anne looked up the local FBI office and placed a call. The office kindly faxed a copy of Mr. Stone's badge with his picture.

Mary Anne escorted Mr. Stone into my office; I greeted him, shook the extended hand, and asked if he would like coffee, tea, or muffins.

"Thank you; I would appreciate a black coffee," He said. Mary Anne quickly brought in coffee and exited, closing the door.

"Ms. West, I am here to ask for your help. It concerns one of your clients, Mr. Nathanial Harris."

"Agent Stone, I will help you in any way I can. Please call me Maye."

We both paused, ostensibly to sip coffee but, in reality, to observe each other. Ward's well-cut suit hid his shoulder harness but revealed the body of a man adhering to a consistent workout schedule. His trimmed coal-black hair blended with piercing black eyes, set in a square-jawed face.

I would have appreciated Frank mentioning that Mr. Stome would be visiting me. I would have worn a suit and tamed my touseled red hair, and a little makeup wouldn't have hurt.

He said, "Thank you; please call me Ward." He smiled, and his face softened. "Maye, Mr. Harris is a person of interest in an investigation. You helped him purchase the home at 4836 W. Columbine Ave. in Peoria. Is that right?"

"Yes, he came to my open house at 3825 West Columbus Drive in West Peoria, saying he wanted to purchase the home on Columbine Drive. He had already made a deal with the seller and just wanted me to write it up."

"And did you do that for him?"

"Yes, but not the way he proposed, that had lawsuit written all over it! I helped him purchase the house legally. Between Viv at Capital Title and Maxmillian Snell, my lawyer, we closed escrow two weeks ago."

"I am curious. How did you pull that off?" He said. Assuming he could subpoena the files, I answered him.

"I wrote a listing and a lease option, Nate came in with the agreed-upon option money, and everything went smoothly. He is planning to apply for a loan. Hopefully, he will qualify by giving him credit for his option money and a portion of the lease amount.

"Do you know where he got that amount of cash? That must have surprised you."

"Yes, it did, and when Nate laid an envelope full of $100 bills totaling

$30,000.00 on Viv's desk. The look on her face was priceless. Nate is a hairstylist with a chair at his wife Naomi's salon and does handyman work. His parents own Harris Construction in Chicago, and he told me he worked for his Father until he struck out on his own and moved to Phoenix. I have a contract with Harris Construction to do the addition to my offices. Will there be a problem with that?"

"No, you can proceed with your construction, but under no circumstances reveal to Nathanial or his parents that he is under investigation. Do you know the salon's address?"

"Yes, it is in his file."

"Maye, I appreciate your cooperation. I will need a copy of your file and the addresses of the Harris family," He said, handing me one of his business cards.

I called Mary Anne and asked her to make copies of everything in Nate's file. Mary Anne returned a few minutes later with two files, a copied file and my original one, and laid them on my desk, quickly exiting.

"Everything is in order. I will review the file with the Attorney General of Arizona. Unless she rules against allowing the lease option, you can proceed. I will caution you again: do not tell anyone of our conversation.

"Ward, by necessity, I must keep Mary Anne, my office manager, in the loop. Frank Singleton of the Sheriff's Department is a friend, and Viv Appleton of Capital Title escrowed the file. They will not divulge any information.

"That will be fine, Maye; thank you for your cooperation."

The minute Ward left my office, Mary Anne opened the door."

"What's going on? Why was the FBI here? Are we in trouble?" She huffed; she must have sprinted from her desk to mine.

"Mary Anne. Sit down, and I will tell you everything. You must promise not to discuss this with anyone outside this office or with anyone, period."

"Okay, okay! I promise, scouts honor," She held up her hand with the proper

signal. Mary Anne's actions were so cute; she reminded me of Lavonne.

My God, if this keeps up, I will be surrounded by Lavonne wanna-be's!

I told her everything. She had a hard time believing Nate could be under suspicion of a crime. I had a creepy feeling running up my spine that this case and my sale were tied together. I stressed the necessity of keeping quiet about this, as the FBI and the Attorney General could cancel the sale, and I wanted to close this sale.

"Alright! I admit it! The commission would be two-fold: a listing, a sale to Nate, another listing, and possibly a sale to another purchaser."

Mary Anne returned to her desk, and I sat thinking about how fast this business could turn from peaches and cream to "Shit on a shingle!" Throwing my feet up on my desk, I leaned back in my chair with my hands behind my head. I mulled over the mess I could be in when all I wanted to do was help a nice young man purchase the house he loved and, yes, make a little money. Okay, a lot of money! I closed my eyes, agonizing over every detail of the transaction, making sure I didn't miss anything or make any mistakes.

When Frank stepped into my office, I pushed work aside and greeted him with a smile. "Hello, Frank, a visit in the middle of the day. How come I don't smell burgers and fries?"

"Business first, burgers, fries, and pleasure later. I take it you had a visit from Ward Stone this morning!"

"Yes, how come you didn't give me a heads up?"

"He asked me not to, and you met him, so you understand, I did as he asked."

"Yes, he just left a few minutes ago. I was sure he knew the answers to all the questions he asked, and I cooperated fully. Mary Anne made a copy of everything in Nate's file. I am allowed to talk to you, Mary Anne, Viv, and Max if he is alive." I paused, taking a breath before asking, "Is he alive?"

"We got confirmation this morning that the murdered man in Max's office was Shawn McGarrett. Max should be back in town tomorrow. But I suspect sooner."

"Fair warning! Max is hell on wheels. He will insist on knowing everything!"

"I cleared it with Ward, and I would be grateful to have you set in on our meeting."

"Thanks, I will be happy to. Just let me know when and where. BTW! When construction begins, have you considered how our little arrangement will suffer? So far, only Mary Anne has 'outed' us. The Harrises and Ed are curious. Oh! And Lavonne is suspicious! We'd better make arrangements soon, or the whole world will know. Maybe you should move back into your Condo for the duration, and I will camp out here in my office. I have the couch, a bath, and a closet, so I'm good."

"Maye, that couch won't be big enough for both of us; the best solution is for you to move into the Condo with me," He said with a shit-eating grin on his face.

"Frank, are you ready to let the whole world know we are a couple?"

"We are, aren't we? I am not seeing anyone else, are you?"

"You know I'm not!"

"So, what's the problem?"

"You know Lavonne, as well as I do, she will have us walking or riding down the aisle with her." Dropping my head into my hands, I moaned, "What are we going to do. We are damned if we do and damned if we don't."

"How about you let me handle this? After all, as Father of the Bride, I can talk with her."

"You are dreaming! When has she ever listened to you or me? She will bat those big blue eyes and say pleeease, and we both will cave. Are we ready for everybody to know about our arrangement?"

"To hell with what anyone thinks; we are adults capable of making our own decisions. Hey, maybe the couch opens up into a bed. If it does, we can tell everyone to mind their own damn business and just camp out right here!" Frank yanked the cushions off the couch, throwing them in various directions! Damn, it did open up to a full-sized bed! We both looked at it and together said, "Ah, Ha," and burst into laughter.

Mary Anne buzzed, "Max is here. Shall I send him in?"

"Show him to the breakroom and make sure he has coffee and treats.

Frank and I will join him shortly.

"How the hell did he get here so fast?" Frank asked.

"I don't know, but he is here, and we had better bust our buts to get in there before he breaks down my door!"

The minute we walked into the room, Max engulfed me in a bear hug, lasting for several minutes. "Maye, darlin', are you okay?" said a muffled voice, sounding far away. He released me to man-hug Frank, not giving me a chance to answer. Eyeing the treats and coffee over Frank's shoulder, he released Frank, proceeded to load a plate with goodies, and fixed his coffee with cream and sugar.

Catching my breath, I said, "Of course I am, Max; the important question is, how are you?"

He paused, holding a doughnut in mid-air, frowning, tossing it on his plate. "Maye, I have been out of my mind, trying to wrap my head around Shawn being dead. I took the red-eye back last night!"

Max is a take-no-prisoners shark lawyer in the courtroom, but he is a teddy bear around his friends, and I could see my friend bravely holding back tears. He spit out, "What the hell happened? One of my agents spent the morning reviewing our files, and I have that list for you, Frank. It doesn't make sense; we do very little criminal work, so it never occurred to me to install more security than good solid locks."

"Max, we believe the break-in at your office was to learn where Wanda Poole is hiding. It appears that anyone that had anything to do with Clarence's wife is in danger." Frank said.

"I came to that conclusion, myself, after the request for that list, but it can't be Clarence Poole; he is in prison! If it wasn't him, I can't for the life of me imagine who it could be! I have been scratching my head; this makes no sense." He said as he slumped in a chair.

I took his hands in mine, "Max, it probably was someone Clarence knew either in prison or connected to his business. There was no way you could have foreseen or prevented this."

"I know, Hon, but I still feel guilty as hell!" He handed Frank a list of possible suspects. "I can't imagine any of these people could do this. Any one of them could be guilty of a time-consuming lawsuit, but not murder!" Max said, rubbing his hand through his imaginary hair.

"I agree with you; the list is to rule them out. My focus is Clarence Poole and anyone associated with him in and out of his business. We have started background checks on his business's current and former employees. Have you ever had any dealings with his business in a legal or personal capacity?"

"Until I compiled this list, I would have said no, but there are a couple of names that you may want to pay close attention to. I marked them with red Xs along with a short explanation."

"Thanks, that will be helpful," Frank put the list in his pocket and, getting up, said, "I will see you later; I need to get this to the office so Shirl and Brenda can start working on it. I will notify Viv and James and have her make sure the information she has at her office is secure. Good seeing you, Max, and thanks again."

I stopped Frank before he could bolt out the door. "Frank, I will be seeing

Viv, this afternoon on other business. I can do the notification for you." He said thanks and hurried out of the office.

I knew Max wanted to know what happened, but I didn't reveal the gory details of the two murders. Knowing they were connected was enough for him to bear. Helping Shawn's widow make arrangements would keep him busy for several days.

"Max, keep the evening of the 17th open; you and Margery are invited to dinner at Butches. Lavonne is in town and is supposed to reveal the nonsense she has dreamed up for her wedding in June to John Kinney. We have reserved the Library. You did a great job with the legal work, and if the interest rates get much higher, we may need you to help to do more of them."

Maye, for you, Darlin,' Marge, and I will be there with bells on." He said but thought, *"Margery and I will need a night out with friends."*

"Great, we will see you there."

"I had better go; Marielle has been notified by now and will need our help making arrangements." He hugged me again and planted a kiss on my forehead before he grabbed a muffin and headed out the door.

I grabbed my purse and stopped by Mary Anne's desk, saying, "If anyone calls for me, take a message. I will be with Viv at Capital Title," waving as I ran out the door.

When I got to Capital Title, I found Viv reviewing closing statements. Looking up, seeing it was me, she happily took a break. I closed her office door and sat in the chair beside her desk.

"Maye, what a surprise! Do you have another juicy escrow?" She said, with a big smile that quickly faded at the look on mine. She sat forward, opening her bottom drawer, holding up a bottle of Yukon Jack. "Shall I pour?"

"I don't know; we might need one or two after I tell you about my visitor this morning and give you some information about our options deal." She set the bottle and the glasses on her desk and looked at me quizzically.

"I had a visit this morning from the FBI. Agent, Ward Stone. He is working with the Phoenix Police and Sherrif's Department and asked me for all my information on Nate Harris. You will probably have a visit from him later today, too!"

"What!"

"Our option transaction is associated with the death of Wanda Poole's neighbor and Shawn Garrett, Max Snell's partner."

"Oh, my God! Maye, I only did the title work! Am I in danger? The deer in the headlights look on her face told me I needed to stay awhile.

She splashed a shot in each glass. Yukon Jack is sipping whiskey liquor, but we both took a generous drink.

"Viv, you knew that Clarence said he would get even with everyone that helped Wanda in any way. We thought those were idle threats as he was in prison. We now know Clarence has someone on the outside trying to find out where Wanda is hiding. Someone broke into Max's office, and poor Shawn McGarrett was mistaken for Max and was killed. Viv, as far as we know, you are the only other person with the information Clarence wants!"

"I am here in Frank's place to tell you and hopefully keep you from panicking, but I can see that ship has sailed!" Viv finished the rest of her drink in one swallow. She poured us another as I continued, "The police are watching everyone, but the main thing I wanted to find out is, are you still packing, and how secure is your safe?"

She picked up the glass and emptied it again in one gulp.

"Maye, you know I pack! I may not be as accurate as you, but I do okay. I can handle being visited by the FBI, too!

"Ward Stone is a by-the-book agent, and trust me, he will know the answers before he asks the questions."

"Oh hell, will I have cops under my feet all the time? Wait a minute, you said the cops will be watching us. Is James in danger? My God, Maye, you are in danger too!"

"Viv, remember I have an in-house cop? And I never leave home without my gun."

When the second glass hit her system, she calmed down and put the bottle and glasses away.

I decided to stay with her for a bit longer. I could see she was a little unnerved but holding it together until the receptionist notified her that she had a visitor. It just happened to be Mr. Ward Stone. I left her with a strong cup of black coffee in her hands, not looking happy but calmer.

Chapter 6 Is Clarence in prison? OMG, a Dude Ranch!

My little apartment was about to undergo an upgrade! Relaxing in the relief-giving jet streams of my hot tub, for the last time, I felt a slim body slide in beside me.

"Hello, stranger, what brings you to my humble abode?" I said, looking into the handsome face of my lover.

"I was on the way to my condo when my truck turned around all by itself, and I ended up here naked beside you!"

"That is strange because I was sitting here wishing you were here, and naked is a plus. My powers of persuasion must be stronger than I realized." I said. We snuggled closer.

"Man, being apart for the months of construction will be tough on both of us," I mumbled.

"Maye, we are two grown-up individuals, and we can make up our minds about our sleeping arrangements!"

"Okay, the hell with the entire world," I said, splashing him.

"I Agree!" He said, returning the favor. After we splashed a sufficient amount of water to satisfy our inner children, we enjoyed grown-up lovemaking.

The next morning at breakfast, Frank reminded me, "Maye, things have been too quiet; I don't think for a minute Clarence is giving up. I am certain this is the lull before the storm. He wants to find his ex-wife, and I am damn sure he has more than one plan in the works."

"Frank, you need to be careful; we just started this new arrangement, and I want to try it out a bit longer!"

"I promise I won't take any chances," Frank said with a faraway look on his face. "You know, the warden assured me Clarence is still in prison, but I did not personally see him in prison. What if that isn't Clarence in the cell? Could he have changed places with someone else during the attempted jailbreak? I need to make damn sure that the person in his cell is Clarence! I am going to find out for certain today!" After a quick cup of coffee, Frank disappeared.

When Frank got to his office, he rang warden John Grissom. He asked to visit the prison, getting a yes; he called Ward Stone and asked if he wanted to go with him. Ward arrived at the Sheriff's office on Jefferson St. in twenty minutes. They headed south on I-10, turned east on Route Eighty-Seven to Florence, and pulled into the Prison parking lot. They were escorted to the Warden's office.

"Mr. Grissom, thanks for seeing us on short notice; this is Ward Stone, FBI liaison with our department on this case."

John said, "Good to meet you, Mr. Stone, Mr. Singleton. What can I do for you today?"

"We drove down today to verify that Clarence Poole is, in fact, the man incarcerated in this prison."

"Do you have reason to believe that it is not Poole?"

"Clarence threatened to kill his ex-wife and anyone that helped her. There have been two murders of people connected to her; if he couldn't commit these crimes, it must be someone he knew or someone that worked for him."

Frank handed the files to the warden; he opened the first one, looked at the pictures for a second, took another quick view of the second folder, and said, "What do you need?"

"I brought his picture taken at the time of his arrest; we would like to compare it to a recent picture."

Warden Grissom handed Frank a picture from Clarence's file. Both he and Ward compared the photos.

"It certainly looks like the same man! Can we get a good close-up look at him in person?" Ward asked.

"I can do better than that; I will show you a live video; he is in the exercise yard. I can highlight him and show you a close-up." He said, smiling.

John zoomed in as Clarence looked up, and they agreed he looked like the same man. Ward said, "Can we arrange to take fingerprints and a DNA test to compare with our database."

John arranged to bring Clarence to an observation room with one-way glass. He had his officers take the sample and fingerprints.

Frank and Ward thanked John and left for the 61-mile drive back to Phoenix.

Ward said, "Hey, there's a Wendys; pull over, and I will treat you to a burger and fries."

"Okay, as long as it includes a chocolate Frosty!"

"You got it!"

Frank pulled off the highway and pulled into Wendy's parking lot.

"Clarence wasn't a happy camper getting his DNA and fingerprints taken!" Ward stated.

"No, he fought it tooth and nail; it was kinda fun to watch."

"I felt his eyes boring into me, even though he couldn't possibly see through the one-way glass."

They finished their lunch and got back on the road to Phoenix.

Ward immediately left to run the sample and, within two hours, was back to compare the results with the evidence of both crime scenes.

They both agreed that unless he had an identical twin brother, the person in that cell was, in fact, Clarence Poole!

"Someone else is doing Clarence's dirty work, or there is a different reason for the two murders. We looked at everyone on Max's list and are back to square one. Didn't you say you were investigating everyone that works for Clarence?" Frank said.

"My department is looking at everyone working for him now that shared his cell, or he knew in prison, and any visitors," Ward said.

"That would be great," Frank said; they shook hands, and Ward left.

Ward was only gone a minute, and there was another knock, "Come in."

James Crandall wasn't a happy camper. He paced the floor in front of Frank's desk, leaning into Frank's face, saying, "What the hell is going on? Viv came home yesterday, clearly frightened. She told me she was the only one who knew that woman's address, and two people have already been murdered. How much danger is Viv in? What are you doing to keep her safe?"

Frank stood up, leaning in, so he was face to face, and said, "James, I wish I could tell you she isn't in danger, but I won't lie to you. She and Max are the only people who know where Wanda Poole is hiding. Maye knew Clarence was in prison but had no idea he was a serious threat when she wrote the option contract! Viv told you that the FBI is helping with our investigation, didn't she?"

"Yes, but how many people are in danger?"

"Max, Maye, Viv, for sure, and anyone that had access to her files."

"What are you doing to ensure their safety?"

"We have officers watching everyone 24/7, and the FBI has undercover agents watching the major players, like Viv, Max, and Maye.

James appeared to deflate and sat back down. Frank sat down, too.

"Your job will be to stay close to Viv. And stay off the lake, no, fishing or hunting, until we solve this thing."

"That shouldn't be a problem; I am asking Viv to marry me tonight. We will be busy for the next two or three weeks. Our house is being remodeled by Mi and Josh as a wedding present! It will give us room when the family comes to John and Lavonne's wedding. OMG! I just realized the murders will be big news! When John hears about them and the connection to us, he will be out of his mind with worry. What am I going to tell him? Should they call the whole thing off?"

He fumed as he paced the floor until another idea popped into his head, and he exploded, "What do we know about the Harris's? Especially that, Nat kid?"

James, we are looking into everyone that could be involved. I promise you, "Viv's safety is our priority, but her safety may depend on you, too, James." Frank said, ignoring the question about Nate.

"No problem. I will take Viv to work every day, eat lunch with her, and drive her home."

Hearing Frank answer his questions truthfully, James felt satisfied Frank was doing everything he could do to keep everyone safe and left to assume his duties of protecting the woman he loved

Late in the afternoon, or more accurately about dinner time, Ward returned with the test results taken at the prison. They confirmed that Clarence was not the killer unless he could walk through walls.

"Frank, I apologize for not having the other two lists ready yet, but I will have them tomorrow."

"You just got them; take time to breathe, Ward; even Feds need to take time to live. Hey, I've got an idea. Why don't you and your wife join us at Butch's Restaurant this Saturday at 7:00. We are celebrating the office remodel, new friends, and Maye's best friend, Lavonne Hall, is revealing the wedding plans."

"I wouldn't want to intrude on a personal celebration."

"You've met most of the guests, and Butch always cooks for us. If that maniac Clarence makes an appearance, it might be a different kind of celebration.

Another gun or two would be welcome. Please come!"

"When you put it that way, I accept your invitation. My wife, Candy, is an agent, too, and we have wanted to try Butch's for some time."

Grinning, Frank said, "This will be Butch's best-protected party! By the way, Maye reserved the Library."

"We have heard about it, and Candy will be thrilled. Thanks, we will be there."

Ward took his leave, and Frank got back to worrying about Maye.

As promised, Ward returned the next day and laid a stack of thick folders on Frank's desk.

"Here is information on every person who worked with Clarence in his shop, his salespeople, and his relatives. We contacted Warden Grissom and got a list of everyone who occupied Clarence's cell with him. He also included all the guards that had any connection with him and the medical personnel."

Before he opened a file, Frank said, "Did you include all of Maye's and my friends too?"

"We have files on most of them; I will bring those tomorrow!" He was so straight-faced that Frank sat there in shock.

Ward burst out laughing! "The look on your face is priceless!"

"Man, you're gonna fit right in at the party in the Library!"

"I assigned Agents to anyone that might pose a problem. You should keep your vigilance concentrated on your friends. What precautions have you taken for the party? That would be a good time for them to make a move. Will anyone besides you be carrying?"

"The ones I am sure of are Maye, Viv, John, James, and my two deputies.

Unfortunately, Maye is the most dangerous! You may have heard about Maye's Annie Oakley's performance last year at Mi and Josh's open house."

"Yes, I have! You are one lucky man! I read the report; I know another woman like her, named Candy Stone." Ward paused with a big grin, saying, "It looks like our women can protect us; we might as well relax and leave our guns at home."

"Not on your life! Your wife is an agent; the brass didn't take too kindly to a civilian shooting the bad guy right between the eyes!"

"Arpaio must have thought it was a hoot! I am surprised Maye didn't get a commendation."

"He didn't go that far, but the paperwork was a bitch!"

"Yeah, I know there are miles of forms. Thanks for the invite. Candy is thrilled!"

Frank called to tell me about Ward and Candy; it would be interesting to see Ward in a different setting.

Lavonne was working on decorating my office and apartment and was flitting in and out every day. No matter how many times I pleaded with her, no cutesy crap, she would not show me the plans until I put my foot down and demanded to see them. Looking hurt, she handed them over, knowing full well I wouldn't understand her hieroglyphics. She was right, of course. I didn't understand much! I did see that she kept the same theme, highlighting the vintage and new.

Breathing a sigh of relief, I said, "Lavonne, you are a genius! I love it!" I was skeptical about seeing the plans for my apartment, but I dove right in and said, "Okay, spill it. Explain the plans for my apartment."

"Your appliances are upgraded, and a king-sized bed in your Mistress' bedroom. Another in the second bedroom, along with some new comfortable furniture and a big-screen TV. You will notice I did not touch your hot tub. I added a treadmill, sauna, a weight bench, and some weights."

"Lavonne, you know I don't go for that heavy-duty workout stuff!

"But Frank does!"

"Dammit, she knows! We are outed for sure now!

"That's good. He will like the work out before a tub when he stays over. Thanks, Hon." I said, putting my arms around her.

Maye, you don't have to play innocent with me." She said.

I looked down at her, hoping my expression seemed as blank as I intended it to be. "Lavonne, I haven't been innocent for some time, and you know Frank and I have been friends and lovers, and that is not likely to change."

"Yes, I know that, but I hoped you wouldn't mind if I added a few touches for Frank."

"Of course not; he will like them." I knew I didn't fool her for a minute, but we kept up the farce out of friendship. She flitted off without giving me a chance to question her about her plans for 'la grande ' wedding. I was left in the dark and would stay there until dinner, now only a day away. I tried to keep my imagination in check. Still, my mind raced around several scenarios, each scarier than the last. I was surprised and grateful she hadn't left written details for the outfit and jewelry I was supposed to wear tomorrow night!

Butch arrived to discuss the dinner party, diverting my mind from worrying about Lavonne's plans.

"Maye Darlin', I opened the Library, giving plenty of space for dancing, and arranged the seating with name tags, and here is the dinner menu for you to approve."

The dinner menu was our favorite! Prime Rib, au jus, with steamed veggies and baked Idaho potatoes with mountains of sour cream, butter, and the additions we love. After the perfect dinner, he added a five-layer chocolate cake with his famous chocolate fudge frosting. Butch, himself, would be preparing our meal, and he included bottles of chilled champagne.

"Butch, you left several places blank. Are you planning on joining us with a date?"

"Now, Maye, Darlin', you know I only have eyes for you!" He said, showing that beautiful Butch smile. Butch is a couple of inches taller than me and reminds me of the Pillsbury Dough Boy with a fantastic mustache.

"Sweetheart, it looks terrific, and your restaurant will be well protected tomorrow night. Several guests are law enforcement and will most likely be armed."

"Oh, my word! I will add wanted posters and have my wait staff dress in Western apparel with pistols and ten-gallon hats! He belly laughed until I said, "That might not be a bad idea; there is a good chance that some bad guys might come uninvited to the party."

"Whaaat! I thought you were yanking my chain. Are my guests and I in danger?" He said, visibly shaken. I hugged him with my best bear hug and whispered in his ear, "Butch, honey, I promise I will take care of you, and if I fail, you can depend on Frank!" I held him until he stopped shaking. Of course, he faked nervousness just to get me to hug him longer, and I played along. I was onto his game; he liked the feel of my boobs on his chest. Butch is one of my favorite people, but he knows he could never take Frank's place.

I eased out of his arms, and he left to ensure a cooked-to-perfection meal; I sat back, dreading the bomb Lavonne would drop in my lap in 24 hours.

Saturday night approached so fast that my head was spinning, although it could have been from exhaustion. When sleep finally overtook me after I lay awake most of the night, I dreamed of singing 'Buttons and Bows' and riding a bucking bronco!

I chose a comfortable, conservative outfit, a white long-sleeved blouse, black slacks, and flat-heeled shoes, adding a simple gold necklace and earrings. Frank wore his casual suit cut to hide his shoulder holster. It didn't look Western, but he added a Bola tie. He looked so good I mentally slapped myself to keep from making us late for the party.

Frank noticed me adding my Glock to my purse and said, "There will be plenty of official law enforcement personnel tonight. Do you really need her?"

"Frank, I never leave home without Miranda! What are you worried about?"

"Hon, I am not really worried, but the last time, it took me several days to finish the paperwork." He said with a lopsided grin.

"I promise to shoot, only if it is necessary." He didn't look relieved.

When we arrived, Butch Buxton himself greeted us at the door. He escorted us to the Library where Lavonne and John were whispering but immediately stopped and looked guilty as hell!

We were not surprised to see John, and we both said, "John, glad you could make it tonight!"

"I missed Lavonne so much, and when she told me about the celebration, I hopped on a plane." He said with his arms around her.

We knew better; James must have filled him in on the option house deal and the danger. John's modest western suit, hat, and boots blended with Lavonne's lovely pale blue dress. It had a decided Western flair with lace and ruffles, sending my overactive imagination into hyperdrive. I was sure she had something spectacular planned that spelled danger and humiliation for me. The guys shook hands, and Lavonne hugged me.

James and Viv arrived. She flashed an engagement ring until we all noticed and gathered to congratulate them. They downplayed wedding plans, not wanting to overshadow John and Lavonne's big surprise. James wore a western suit and a pair of well-tooled western boots, a gift from his son John. Viv blended with him in a lovely beige dress, a lace ruffle around the low neckline, and plain brown pumps.

Shirl Packard arrived in a western outfit, hiding his shoulder holster, complete with cowboy boots. Brenda Brannen's service gun was resting in a western holster riding on her hip, and her dress had crocheted lace around the hem, touching twins to Shirl's boots. Brenda took her Texas cowboy hat off and expertly sailed it across the room, settling it on a hook. Everyone clapped in appreciation.

Ed and Kaye arrived and joined in the greeting with hugs. If I didn't know better, it appeared that Ed was starting to like the hugs. He wore a black suit with a western-themed tie, and Kaye's deep green dress had small gold beads sewn around the neck, accentuating her red hair.

Max and Margery Snell walked in. Max struck a commanding presence as usual with his shining bald head, black mustache, and charming curl. His black suit encompassed his tall, substantial frame, contrasted by an almost neon-red tie. He towered over and out-shown petite Margery in her plain pink dress.

Ward made his presence known with his gorgeous wife Candy in her white sheath over a runway model figure and Black hair touching her shoulders and framing her perfect face. Looking at them, I couldn't help thinking, *"Barbie and Ken" came to the party.*

The couple that took the prize was Al and Mich Harris! Mich, a striking woman with large brown eyes, a short afro, and nary a wrinkle on her beautiful face, and her pale gray dress revealed her great shape. Al also sported a short afro sprinkled with gray; his well-cut dark blue suit showed he did manual labor. Amanda Harris proudly held their hands, dressed in a full-skirted sparkling dress, the color of her bright blue eyes. Her milk chocolate complexion with long, curly, light brown hair with blonde highlights complemented her beautiful face.

Nate got into the Western theme, sporting a well-fitting western suit and Aligator-leather cowboy boots. His huge smile showed off his dark complexion, short afro, and sparkling eyes. Naomi's deep blue silk off-the-shoulder dress with pale blue lace around the neckline matched her pale blue eyes, contrasting with her pale skin and almost white hair,

Mi and Josh arrived, prompting several minutes of greetings and hugs. She was beautiful in a simple black sheath dress, setting off her lovely black eyes and hair. The white fur stole wrapped around her shoulders and framed the picture. Josh was sporting a tweed jacket with leather elbow patches, looking like the successful author he now was!

The group's lively discussion centered on everything but the two murders out of respect for Max.

Butch entered the room, announcing, "Dinner is served!" He was wearing his usual outfit of a white full-sleeved shirt with a silk brocade waistcoat over Black slacks. His wait staff got in the cowboy/cowgirl theme with vests and black pants, white shirts, hats, and brocade vests matching Max's. They opened bottles of champagne and expertly poured them for everyone. Mi proposed a toast about good friends, and we cheered as we reflected on our diverse group's friendship.

We were seated at our designated places with name tags supplied by Butch. The wait staff trouped in with vegetables, potatoes, sour cream, and hot bread with fresh butter. Before we could indulge, Butch himself emerged ahead of the aroma of perfectly cooked prime rib adorning a large platter covered with a silver dome. He expertly carved the roast to each person's desires. Butch covered the remaining slices with the insulated dome, keeping it warm and fresh for seconds if desired.

What I love about the Library is privacy. The art, and the collection of leather-bound classic books, soothes my soul. The Highly polished shelves and the dark mahogany wood wainscoting complete an old English country estate atmosphere.

Sated, we sat back in our seats, relaxing and sipping champagne. The room became quiet. My hope against hope that Lavonne had forgotten about her big announcement was short-lived when they exclaimed, "We have some exciting news! You remember John and I became engaged last fall at Mi and Josh's housewarming. We decided to have our wedding and reception at a lovely place in North West Arizona on June 10th. We have reserved the entire Stagecoach Trails Guest Ranch for our wedding party, using the chapel or an evening ceremony in the garden."

There were sighs of approval, imagining glowing lanterns under the stars and a quaint chapel. Lavonne and John looked so smug and happy.

My silent protests went unnoticed by everyone excitedly asking questions. John and Lavonne declared, "Hold on to your hats! We have all the information in these packets for you." John placed a stack of large white envelopes emblazoned with the Stagecoach Trails Guest Ranch logo on the front table and handed them to everyone. I glanced through my booklet long enough to realize her lovely place was a working Dude Ranch! What the hell am I going to do? I have only been on a horse once in my life!

Frank gave me the 'say nothing you will regret' look, and I kept my mouth shut for once.

"This Dude Ranch has 360,000 acres of natural western desert beauty at the foot of the Mohave and Hualapai mountains with breathtaking views and endless sunny days. It is only 2 hours from Las Vegas and the Grand Canyon and is arranged like an old western town. The owners say you will be transported back in time and live the life of real cowboys and cowgirls. And just for us city dudes, they have a swimming pool, hot tub, hiking, archery, wagon rides, and cowboy action shooting. Each room has a large patio with rocking chairs and some with courtyards. The Western theme is maintained throughout. We can head out to Frontier Lodge for fun or to the large courtyard and watch wranglers demonstrate their roping and bullwhip skills. All this under the stunning sunsets and star-studded sky."

They paused, and I saw that Josh, Mi, Viv, James, Ward, and Candy appeared enthusiastic about this idea. Frank looked way too relaxed about it for my comfort. I sat there smiling like a Cheshire cat, hiding my horror from everyone. I emptied my glass in one swallow and got another, hoping to stupify the obnoxious comments forming in my head. I succeeded only in keeping my opinions on how much I hated the idea while getting a buzz from too much champagne.

Pouring a second glass of Champagne and downing it in one swallow might have given me away. I saw a pair of big blue eyes belonging to my best friend peeking into my mind.

"What's the matter, Maye? I thought you would love the idea of all that fresh air, no crowds, and comfortable clothes."

That statement said nothing about horses, snakes, scorpions, and spiders. "Lavonne, I love the idea of relaxed clothes with no ruffles and bows!"

She didn't bat an eyelash, saying, "I promise there will be none of those." I scanned her face to see if she flinched a little. I relaxed until the group started talking excitedly about the "night on the trail" the Dude

Ranch sponsors yearly. Things like "sleeping on the ground, eating pork and beans, and biscuits cooked over the fire, whirled around in my head like a hurricane. Frank noticed my face as pale as a ghost,

I gave him a big, forced smile but said nothing. The only good thing about the evening's announcements was the bad guys didn't show up, and they were lucky; my mood would have spelled danger for them and tons of paperwork for Frank.

Frank would understand why horses petrified me and wouldn't say something stupid like, "Just get over it!" He might suggest a get-acquainted time with gentle horses and riding lessons. But I knew the horror would return the minute I got within 10 feet of one of those massive beasts.

The drive home felt like a hundred miles, and I could hear the laughter in my head when the entire wedding party learned I was a wuss.

Frank didn't say a word when we entered the apartment, and he suggested we shower and relax in the hot tub. Once we were comfortable in the soothing bubbles, he broached the subject.

"Maye, I know you pretty well, and the thought of horseback riding petrified you. Are you ready to tell me why?"

"Frank, I have had exactly one experience riding a horse, and I plan on it being my last!"

"I am sorry, Hon. What happened? Did you get thrown?"

"If getting thrown was what happened, it would be no problem, but horses are as vicious as their owners! Stay there; I need to show you something."

"What?"

"My back!"

"I love your backside." He said with a lopsided grin.

I got out of the tub and turned on the lights, and when I turned my back to him, he gasped.

"Getting thrown from a horse did that?"

"No, being dragged across a field did! I was barefoot, and the horse and saddle were way too big for me. You know I am vertically challenged now, but I had reached my maximum height at age 10. A friend asked me to ride with her, and she made it sound so much fun. I imagined myself galloping across the desert, the wind blowing my hair. My first clue should have been leading the horse to a barrel so I could mount it. My bare feet didn't quite reach the stirrups. We started off at a slow walk, and everything was hunky-dory.

"My friend took off at a gallop, and my horse took off too! I don't think I stayed in the saddle for more than a minute. I woke up with a concussion; my shoulders scraped raw. The hair on the back of my head took a year to grow back. She thought it was a hoot seeing me dragged with my foot caught in the stirrup! She finally stopped laughing and caught the damned horse! Her parents were scared shitless of being sued and paid for everything."

"What am I going to do? I am petrified of horses! I can hardly breathe within 10 feet of one. At Amanda's party, there was a pony, and I didn't step off the patio!"

"Maye, you are the bravest woman I know. Did you ever get any counseling?"

"No, in those days, it was not an option. Over the years, I have managed to stay away from horses. Frank, I can't say no to Lavonne! What am I going to do?"

"Honey, relax; we will work something out. It surprises me that Lavonne doesn't know? You two have been friends forever!"

"You are the only person that has ever seen my back!"

"Maybe it would be good to tell Lavonne; she loves you enough to change or modify her plans.

"I know she does, but I can't ask her to change her dream wedding plans."

"I know you can't, but I promise we will find a way for you to enjoy the romance of the Western wedding without going near a horse."

"I knew you would be on my side. Thank you for loving me."

"You are welcome, ma'am." He said in his best cowboy voice.

Chapter 7 Mary Anne has a visitor!

The next morning, the construction crew arrived, and all day, I removed earplugs and put them back in again. Even though it was music to my ears to get my office remodeled, it was loud.

Late morning, Fast Eddie entered my office, closed the door, and, taking off his noise-canceling headphones, said too loud, "This is not working for me, Maye; I am going to head home and work!"

"No problem, I would do that too, but it wouldn't help."

Laughing, he said, "I need to talk to you. Kay and I have talked it over, and I will semi-retire for a while. If you allow me to work part-time, I will happily come in and get files ready for audit."

"Eddie, it has always been a big help for you to take on that job. I understand and will happily have you continue, but may I ask why?"

"Kaye has some health issues. It's nothing major, but I want to be around home more. I will come in regularly to review new files and keep them current. I will still do a couple of deals a year for friends. I will start next week, taking a box of files home and return them ready for audit. Eventually, I will come in once or twice a month to update them. If Is that okay with you?"

"Ed, you don't even have to ask. It won't be the same without you here; you have been my right hand for so long. But promise me one thing? If I get roped into another big deal, I can call on you to help? I will miss being able to knock on your door with problems, but I understand and will be happy to have you here as much as you can. I only have one request, please leave your headphones with me today."

"I will clean out my office, giving you room for new agents. And no problem with borrowing my headphones during the remodeling,"

"Thanks. I don't think I can grin and bear it without them."

I got up and came around the desk, and we hugged. "Ed, I am not saying goodbye because you will still hang out here periodically. Your license will remain current, and you will have an office when you decide to go full-time again."

Ed hugged me again, and he left, both a little teary-eyed.

I asked Mary Anne to come into my office. We sat with coffee and discussed how the office is growing with agents and the safety of our files.

"Maye, many of the offices are locking their files, and agents need permission to look at them once they are in escrow or closed; of course, most good agents keep a copy at home. Having them available for anyone other than the agents involved is dangerous. You, me, and Eddie need access if he is regularly preparing files for audit.

"I don't like it, but I can see the wisdom of keeping them locked."

"We can use the closet behind my desk, but I think it needs to be modified to make it bigger and more secure. You could speak to other Brokers about how they handle locking their files."

"Good idea; I will make some calls and maybe visit an office or two and pick their brains. It will be good to get out of this noise."

"If anyone comes in or calls for you, do you want me to refer them to you or take a message?"

"If Mich comes in or calls, mention locking up our files and show them your closet and mine for ideas. I think I will go to lunch; Butch has been dying for me to visit. During part of the remodel, we will have to close up shop for a day or two because of the mess, and I will take you with me for one of my Champagne and Crab lunches."

"It sounds fabulous. I have heard about Butch stocking half bottles for you."

"Butch pretends to be madly in love with me; he acknowledges my relationship with Frank, but he pursues me anyway, and it's so good for my ego."

"Maye, I have heard he swings for the other team. He sounds fun, and maybe he will pursue me too after I meet him at one of your famous lunches." She was giggling as she left the room.

Between hammering, things falling, and people hollering, I called several of my Broker friends and got a lot of information about the wisdom of locking cabinets and invitations to lunch. One Broker told me, "One of my agents peaked in the files and had her client make a higher offer to steal the sale. It caused a lot of hard feelings." I made a couple of dates for lunch at Butch's, which would make him happy. I longed for the privacy of my apartment and a long soak in the hot tub. I grabbed my purse and headed for Butch's. He would be thrilled that Frank could not join us.

Since Mary Anne was alone, she measured the closet behind her desk. She wrote the measurements on her calendar and the file cabinet size that held the current files. Mary Anne searched online for sturdy metal cabinets with secure locks.

Drawing the front office to scale. Mary Anne realized that moving her desk closer to the front door would expand the closet to the needed size. She also suggested a camera connected to her computer to see who was approaching the door. Head bowed, concentrating on double-checking her measurements. She stood over her desk, keeping her from hearing the front door open. A voice startled her, saying, "Hello, Ms. Noble. May I have a minute of your time?"

She stood up so fast she lost her balance, grabbing the desk for support; she looked up at an unfriendly smile. The man was tall; his piercing eyes and the telltale bulge in the shoulder area of his suit put her on guard.

"Good morning; how may I help you? I can ring Maye, and she can be here

in a few minutes." She said, keeping her voice professional.

"That won't be necessary; I would like to discuss a mutually beneficial matter with you."

Mary Anne sat down slowly, quietly opening her bottom drawer and moving her chair close to the desk. "Sir, I am the receptionist. I don't know what you could need from me."

"I need access to your files, and I am aware that part of your job is to protect those files, but it doesn't need to be at the expense of your life." He said with that same unfriendly smile.

"If you are threatening me, it is working!" She said with a voice that she hoped would tell him she was scared out of her wits.

"Ms. Noble, you made a wise and healthy decision. You will give me the information I seek, and in return, I will compensate you very well." Reaching into his jacket pocket, he produced a thick envelope and laid it on her desk.

Looking at the envelope on her desk, she said, "I don't understand!"

"Open the envelope, and I will tell you what you will give me in return for its contents."

Mary Ann leaned forward to retrieve the envelope and, at the same time, retrieved her gun from her purse, carefully aiming it under the desk at his family jewels.

"Sir, would you please put your hands flat on my desk and remain very still! I am reluctant to shoot off a man's balls unless it is absolutely necessary!" Her voice no longer sounded shaky, but like a woman, that meant business. She cocked her head and smiled.

"Now, little lady, that is not necessary! I am trying to conduct a legitimate business transaction!" He said as he moved his right hand slowly toward the bulge in his jacket.

He stiffened and jumped back, swearing, "Son of a Bitch!" As a bullet whizzed by his ear, halting his movement and encouraging him to stand stock-still!

"Now, if you don't mind, please put those hands on my desk while I call a friend at the Sherrif's office to have a chat with you." She said, looking him in the face, not raising her voice.

He did as he was told and didn't move a muscle. Before Mary Anne could dial the number, she heard Nate and Al running through the back of the building, shouting, "What the hell is going on? Was that a shot we heard?"

Mary Anne shouted, "Don't come any closer, just call Frank and tell him to please hurry!" She didn't move a muscle, which prompted the man in front of her not to move either.

To Mary Anne, it seemed like hours before Frank arrived, clamping handcuffs on the man. Searching him, finding two guns. He was put in a car headed to headquarters for booking.

Mary Anne quietly put her pistol back in her purse.

"Mary Anne, are you all right?" All three men said at once.

"I am fine; I haven't had a chance to target practice for months. I hope I didn't damage anything when I fired my gun to get his attention." She said with a straight face.

"Nothing we can't fix as good as new." Al and Nate said together, with smiles a mile wide."

Frank said, "Mary Anne, you'll need to come to the station to make a statement."

"Frank, I don't want to call Maye away from a much-needed relaxing lunch at Butch's. Is it necessary? I can type and sign a statement and have it in your hands before you get this guy to the station."

"You know what, tomorrow will be okay. I think Maye will agree; you should close the office and take the rest of the day off?"

"That sounds nice, but someone needs to be here to protect the workers." She said, grinning at Al and Nate.

Al said, "Ma'am, would you do me the honor of taking time to have lunch with us, two gentlemen? We are buying."

"Thank you; I will be delighted. I would like to show you some plans for the remodel of my office. And if it will not violate the office policy, I would like a stiff drink."

Al said, "Under the circumstances, I agree and think bending the rules is a good idea; we both will join you."

Frank left hearing laughter; he thought, "*She is one cool lady!*"

Mary Anne took her purse and the sketches, and after locking the front door, she followed the men to the break room. Al looked around the kitchen for food but found nothing appealing. While Nate mixed her a drink, Al looked over the sketches and said, "With this sketch, Mich can prepare a solid plan for the remodel; this is a great idea! But, Mary Anne, I have to know how did you stay so calm?"

"I worked part-time in my husband's construction business and used to make night deposits. Carrying a gun made me feel safer. Today is the first time I fired my gun other than target practice, and I hope it will be the last! I took a calculated risk, getting my gun before he pulled his and disarmed me; the outcome would have been much different." She sat back in her chair, taking a deep, cleansing breath, "Now, if you don't mind, I think I earned that drink, Al!"

Maye was relaxing in one of the intimate half-circle booths at Butch's Restaurant. A smiling Butch served her favorite lunch, a mountain of fresh Crab on an open-face English Muffin smothered in melted sharp Cheddar Cheese. The fun conversation and Butch's adoring looks made her day.

Butch opened a full bottle of champagne, "Darling, we can't survive one of those tiny bottles you usually order. It's been years since you graced my restaurant without that Fred person tagging along. I want you all to myself this afternoon."

She was flattered and enjoyed playing Butch's games. It is a good thing she and Frank were not the jealous types. Maye and Butch consumed half the bottle of champagne and were stuffed with food when Maye's phone rang.

Butch listening to her end of the conversation, was mystified.

"Oh, hi, Frank. I am at Butch's having my usual lunch; what's up?"

"What? OMG, I will head back to the office ASAP! Oh! Wait, I had a little too much champagne to drive. Can you stop by and pick me up?"

"Okay, I will be waiting outside."

Poor Butch looked confused, "I am so sorry, Butch, this has been lovely, but I need to go. A man with a gun accosted Mary Anne at my office. She is okay, and the man is in jail."

"OMG, I'm glad she is okay. I will walk you to the door, but let's do this again soon. I miss your wonderful sense of humor and love hearing your funny stories about Real Estate."

Butch walked me to the door and handed me a large bag of food for the crew. He stayed talking with me, trying to keep me calm until Frank arrived.

The minute I got in the car, I peppered Frank with questions, demanding the whole story. Frank said, "Hon, why don't I just hit the high spots and let Mary Anne tell you the entire story. You will be proud of her; she didn't let him get the information he wanted."

The minute we pulled into my spot in the back of the building, I bolted from the car and raced to the break room, panting, skidding to a stop! I must have had an incredulous look on my face. Her feet in a chair, a pillow behind her back, and holding a margarita sat Mary Anne.

"Mary Anne, are you all right?"

"Of course, I have been well taken care of by my two favorite men." She said with a silly look on her face.

Al was sitting beside her with a drink in his hand, too!

"Are you hungry? We were about to order in."

"Thanks, that sounds wonderful, but I suspect the food in this bag will be enough for all of us, courtesy of Butch, and it smells delicious," Frank said.

Al set the table and unwrapped the food.

Mary Anne padded the seat next to her and said to me, "Sit down, and we can talk. Do you want a drink?"

"Yes, I think I need one, even though Butch and I made a dent in a bottle of Champagne."

A drink appeared from nowhere, and after one sip, I said, "Uhm, this is delicious. Al, you are hired!"

He smiled, "I must confess, Nate mixed a pitcher before he went back outside to work on some measuring for me."

"Okay, you both are hired as my bartenders. Margarita is my favorite drink after Champagné, and this is the best I've had in a long time!"

Turning to Mary Anne, I said, "Okay, girl, tell me everything."

Mary Anne told me the story, and I couldn't help laughing out loud at her matter-of-fact recital.

"I was a little nervous, but I don't like bullies! He tried to bribe me, but I had to do something when he reached for his gun. I suppose I can't have the money, can I?" She said, not cracking a smile.

Al said, "Maye, she was a real Annie Oakley! She had him sitting with his hands flat on her desk, not moving a muscle. All we did was call Frank, and she made us stay outside until he arrived and cuffed the guy. He had two guns!"

Frank saw what Al was unwrapping and said, "Maye, there is more than enough

Crab and Cheddar for all of us."

He took one bite and closed his eyes, sighing, "This is heavenly! I can understand why you enjoy your lunches at Butch's!"

Al called Nate inside. The whole crew sat around the table, talking about Mary Anne's amazing shot, and enjoyed the sandwiches Butch packed for them.

Mary Anne exclaimed, "Maye, I can't wait for that lunch at Butches!"

"He will be thrilled to hear about how you stood up to that bully."

Everyone agreed that this was the best office party ever! They stayed in the break room, sipping Margarita's until evening. Everyone was sent home in taxi's. Maye and Frank climbed the stairs to her, soon to be open to the public viewing apartment to spend a quiet evening.

Chapter 8 A Bed and a Rental Agent

After the day's excitement, Frank and Maye relaxed in the tub and later lounged in pajamas and robes.

"What do you want for dinner, Frank."

"Pizza?"

"Sounds good; I'll make the call while you look for something on Prime or Netflix." I was about to dial when my phone rang, "Hey, Mi, good to hear from you. Sounds great; we were about to order Pizza. Sure, whatever you like will be good for us. We stuffed ourselves on Butch's Crab and Cheddar dish this afternoon. I'll tell you all about our interesting afternoon when you get here," She looked at Frank, and he nodded yes.

"Okay, I will see you in a few minutes."

"How much can we tell them about this afternoon?" I asked Frank.

"We can tell them he wanted information from Mary Anne and was prepared to use force to get it, but she acted cool as a cucumber! I suspect by now she is re-living the whole thing. I hope she can get some sleep. I am afraid from now on, everyone needs to be vigilant until we get to the bottom of how Clarence is pulling this off from prison."

"That should be hunky fucking dory!"

Mi and Josh arrived with two pizzas and beer. Frank sat one opened pizza box on the coffee table, and I added glasses, plates, and forks.

Through bites of pizza, Mi asked, "What's your interesting news? Did it have something to do with your option deal?"

"Yes, indirectly! A well-armed man offered Mary Anne a lot of money to give him information about one of our clients."

"OMG, is she okay?"

"Yes, she is."

"Are you sure? She must have been terrified!"

"She may have been, but he didn't get the information he wanted."

Frank told them the story of how Mary Ann calmly told him to put his hands on her desk, or she would shoot his balls off, and she shot once close to his ear to show him she meant business. They were in shock but impressed.

"Frank, does this mean we are all in danger?" Mi blurted"

"I don't think you two have anything to worry about; you were not involved in the sale! But, you could keep a watch on James' house. Viv was the escrow agent, and a couple of people were watching her office. The FBI and the Sheriff's Department are watching everyone close to this deal. If you see anything unusual, call my office. Josh, it might be a good idea to stay off the lake."

"We should talk to the Sodermans and Fred to be on the watch, too! Frank said.

"Maye, you know James is planning on having John's family stay with him for the wedding, don't you?

"I knew he wanted to, but he only has two bedrooms. They will be a little crowded. Are they planning on camping? The weather should be okay."

"Camping would be fun, but James and Viv asked if they could add a couple of bedrooms and a bath. We felt it would be a good investment, so we decided to give James and Viv the addition as a wedding present. Mich is doing the plans, and Lavonne will be doing the decorating."

"That's nice of you."

We were thinking you will soon have no privacy when they start working, and the noise will be horrendous. Why don't you and Frank stay with us for a few weeks while your apartment is open to prying eyes?"

"Mi, that is nice of you to ask, but I know you value your privacy too! We wouldn't want to impose."

"Maye, you and Frank are family! It wouldn't be an imposition, and we would love the company, wouldn't we, Josh?"

"I would love to get some practice with my crossbow, and we could do a little hunting together. James is worried about Viv, and he takes her to work, has lunch with her, and drives her home. With you staying here, he might relax a little." Josh said.

"The Harris's have assured me that it will only be about a week, maybe two, that my apartment will be open to prying eyes, and I want to stay close to the files when the office is closed."

I can understand that, but where will you sleep? You can't stay at the office?"

"Well, we have a solution. Frank discovered the couch in my office opens into a bed, and there is a full bath and a kitchen downstairs."

Mi looked at Frank and said, "Is this your idea or Maye's? Your feet will hang over the end of the bed and lie on the floor."

"It was mine, but now that you mention it, staying with you might be better. My back votes in favor of that!"

"I didn't think about your height, sorry, Frank. Thanks, guys. We are grateful. It has been a long time since we visited Mr. and Mrs. Soderman and Fred, and my mouth can taste her cookies and bread, and Fred's fresh vegetables will be wonderful."

"You know, I kinda like my small office and never intended to hire more agents. Eddie is semi-retiring but will work part-time. I have had several calls from agents asking about joining my team. If they were all like George Peterson, I would hire ten! I am picky about agents because they are like family, and I need to trust them. George is a seasoned agent, was a broker, and is only working to keep busy. His files are complete; he treats his customers like they are VIPs and his only clients!

One Michael York is all I can and want to handle! He thinks he is hot shit and balks at any training. Fast Eddie tears his hair out, checking his files, and he can't afford to lose much! I have met and worked with agents like Michael. Many of them are no longer in the business, and the state requested they turn in their licenses and find another job."

"Yeah, you do the VIP thing, too! I remember how sweet you were to give me swimming lessons," Mi smirked.

"You devil, I didn't have to twist your arm; you were stripping before I finished talking!"

"Have another beer, Maye. You can tell us all about how you treat your clients; you must have lots of juicy stories," Mi said. Grabbing a beer, she tossed it to me. She looked surprised that I caught it and opened it without any fizz.

"Okay, girls, do I need to get out my handcuffs?" Frank said with a big grin on his face.

Mi and I were having a hard time keeping from spitting beer; we were laughing so hard.

We spent the evening laughing and sharing stories of our chosen professions. None of which can be repeated here! Remember, I told you the truth is stranger than fiction? Well, if walls had ears, they would have been blushing! It was a fun, relaxing evening, and ended too soon.

We were looking forward to sharing more stories when the four of us were roomies.

The next morning promised to be a more peaceful day, with Ed's noise-canceling earphones giving me peace.

Mich walked in, waving to get my attention.

"Hi, Mich, what brings you to my office? Do you have the plans to remodel Mary Anne's desk and closet?"

"Yes, I do, but I was wondering if I should make it bulletproof, not to protect her, but your clients?"

Mary Anne was right behind her and said, "That might be a good idea, but you know I didn't shoot him. Just scared him a little!"

Hugging her, Mitch said, "I am glad you were on the job to protect my men."

Mary Anne hugged back, saying, "Anytime, as long as they treat me with those Margaritas, you are one lucky woman!"

Mary Anne left, and Mitch said, "Maye, I need your help. Al and I enjoy being here so much and have several projects to finish. It looks like we will be staying here for a while. We would like to rent a condo or a house, preferably close to enough to Nate but not close enough to be pests."

"I can't imagine you ever being pests, but staying here will make a certain young lady very happy. No problem, I have a friend who is the best rental agent in the business! She will find what you want and fast! We trade referrals between Sun City and Phoenix's west side. I never go there unless absolutely necessary; I am afraid of getting lost and never finding my way home."

The hammering stopped, and we heard the men come in and heard a noise in the kitchen. By mutual agreement, we decided to check on them. Sure enough, Al was behind the counter, opening the refrigerator and taking out plastic dishes of food. It looked like he was planning on having company for lunch.

"Hi, hon, Maye, are you hungry? We have plenty, ask Mary Anne too, but tell her to leave her gun in her purse." Al said with a big grin.

"I'll ask her, then will make the call to Martha Rhenquist."

Mary Anne said, "I heard what Al said and would love to eat with them. By the way, have you heard from Frank why that man was here?"

"No, but this morning, his attorney showed up and bailed him out." Putting up my hand, stopping her questions, I said, "Let's talk over lunch; I need to call my rental agent for Mich."

I called Martha, and she said she was on my side of town and would drop in later.

Entering the break room, I saw Al and Nate chopping ingredients for a huge salad. Mich and Mary Anne were sitting watching, each with a glass of white wine in her hand. As I sat down next to them, Nate handed me a drink.

"Good news, Martha is on this side of town and will drop in, and you can talk to her. I think she works rentals for me just to get out of Sun City once in a while. It looks like if she gets here soon, there will be plenty of salad for all of us."

"I usually get carried away with salad. Mich says I am a part rabbit," Al said.

"It's a good thing I love it too! We have a greenhouse in our yard in Chicago, and in the summer, we have enough fresh salad fixings for the whole family. Any chance of a portable greenhouse here?"

"In the winter, it probably would work, but in the summer, it might be a challenge; you might talk to some of the gardeners. I can garden almost as well as I can cook."

Mary Anne was about to quiz me about the man who visited her when Frank and Ward walked in.

"Hey, we didn't know there was a party. Can we get an invitation?" Frank said as they pulled up chairs. Al sat two more bowls, forks, and napkins in front of them, saying, "Sure, we have plenty, wine?"

"No wine, but ice water would be great. Don't get up; I'll get it. Relax and eat your lunch."

He no more sat down when Mary Anne asked, "What happened with my visitor? Maye said he is out on bail."

"Yeah, his shyster lawyer showed up the first thing this morning before we could question him again. Although questioning was a dead end since he didn't utter a word, Ward and I kept at him for several hours yesterday afternoon."

"I checked on him through several databases, and he does not have a record anywhere. His lawyer tried to threaten us, telling us we had to arrest Mary Anne for shooting at him. It was a "he said, she said." He won't even get his hand slapped for threatening her because there were no witnesses." Ward said.

"Did any of you see or hear anything?" Frank said, holding up his hand to prevent anyone from saying anything. "No? We can't prove he was reaching for a gun, and there is no evidence of you shooting at him. Mary Anne, you will need to revise your statement. If we checked your gun, would it show evidence that it was fired recently?"

"No, it always is clean." She said.

Al spoke up, with a silly grin on his face, "Mary Anne, I think we will do the remodel on your office before we do any more outside. Mitch has the plans finished, so there is no reason we can't start this afternoon. We will remove the old wall and put a new one closer to the door with room for two chairs if someone is just signing the paperwork. Nate is adding a camera connected to your computer. The door will chime when opened, and you can see anyone coming up the walk."

"Thank you, everyone. I appreciate your help." Mary Anne said.

We finished our lunch and were relaxing and in-breezed Martha Rhenquist, taking everyone by surprise! She looked taller than Frank with her full head of teased white-blonde hair. Her Broadway Show make-up was set off by a bright red suit with a multicolored silk blouse and 6-inch red heels. She stood posing like a candidate running for office

"Maye, darlin', where do the people need a house?"

Before anyone could speak, she walked around the room, shaking everyone's hands and introducing herself. When she got to me, she engulfed me in a hug that lifted me off the floor. When I got my breath, I said, "Martha, this is Mitch Harris. She and her husband, Al, want a house near their son Nate. I will get the address for you; it is in my office." Mitch and Martha followed me to my office so they could talk. I wish I had a video of her entrance and everyone's reaction.

Mitch gave Matha the essential features they wanted, and with her notebook full of notes, she breezed out as fast as she came in, saying, "I'll be back in touch with several places for you to view." Fortunately, she only shook Mich's hand and mine.

When the door shut behind her, Mitch sat still for several minutes and then burst out laughing. As she wiped tears, she asked, "Is she as good as she looks?"

"Yes, she has been a friend of mine for years, and she always looks like she is running for office. She gets the job done and fast. You should get ready to move!"

True to their word, the guys began tearing out the wall as soon as lunch was finished, and by evening, they had expanded the closet ready for paint. The last thing they did was put a new mahogany face on Mary Anne's desk, covering the tell-tale bullet hole.

The Harris crew worked quickly, and all too soon, the day came when we had to pack up and leave my snug apartment. We spent the day packing pictures and wall hangings. The furniture was placed in a storage locker, along with most of my clothes. I put the two dozen files that might close in the next two to three weeks in my attache case to be available if needed. My jewelry was going with me to Mi's and locked in her safe. Ward had my file cabinet taken to his office in downtown Phoenix and locked in a holding cell in the basement.

Frank and I spent our last night in my tiny apartment, enjoying the hot tub for the last time for a week or two. We ordered pizza and drank beer, with our suitcases sitting beside us, waiting for our prolonged stay with Mi and Josh. The last thing Frank said before we fell into bed was, "We are off on a new adventure together."

We slept later than usual and lingered over coffee. Neither of us was hungry, so we kissed goodbye and went our separate ways. I went downstairs to check on the office. My day was pretty dull; my crew was working from home, and there was too much noise and dust to linger. Mary Anne had the phones re-routed to her house and was hopefully getting some rest. I walked around, saying goodbye to my past life, and tried imagining my new life with Frank and me permanently living together.

I shook myself out of my daydream and was a little at odds with no business to do. In a fit of brilliance, I called Lavonne. I invited her to join me at our favorite spa for a mani/pedi and facial. I thought I was so devious, planning to pump her for details of what exactly her western wedding would entail and what she would force Frank and me to wear. Unfortunately, she was ready for me, and it looked like she planned to stay close-mouthed all day.

Dammit!

During the Mani/Pedi's, we talked more than we had in a long time. It might have been the complimentary wine. Lavonne is lightweight, and after two glasses, she became talkative.

I was like a vulture, preparing to pounce on her for information when she said. "Maye, do you remember the time you pleaded with me to take you shopping in Seattle? We had steak and Champagne at Johnnie's at Fife, and after dinner, we drove across the freeway to the Poodle Dog for hot fudge sundaes?"

"Lavonne, your recollection is a little different than mine.! As I recall, you kidnapped me at 6 AM and forced me to go shopping all day!"

She cocked her head and, with an impish grin, said, "It was fun, wasn't it?"

"Yes, of course, it was. I admit, if I didn't have you to pick out my clothes, I would run around in rags."

"And the steak and lobster were wonderful, too, weren't they?"

"Yes, and I loved the huge hot fudge sundae after dinner, too, but not as much as you. Do you remember telling me not to worry because you would be my navigator?"

"And I did a great job, too!"

"Oh, yes, your head hit the window the minute I started the car, and you snored all the way back to Montesano."

"I did not! I might have napped a little."

The gals doing our toes enjoyed our conversation so much that we got the works on our feet, plus a fantastic massage.

I was on a roll and had a head of steam when the gal filled our glasses for the third time; I applied pressure to Lavonne. "Lavonne, don't you think since we have been best friends for a hundred years and I am your stand-in Mother, I should know the wedding details? I might have some ideas for your Western theme. After all, I did grow up on a farm in Maine."

"Maye, you told me that was a 15-acre field surrounded by woods. How can you compare that to a Dude Ranch?"

"Come on, Lavonne, give me something! I am going crazy imagining things. I feel like I am in the movie Scrooge with Christmas's past!"

"Maye, we have been friends forever! Have I ever done anything to hurt or embarrass you?"

I was in trouble here, embarrass me, maybe, but she would never hurt me. I didn't answer her, letting the silence build!

"Maye, I promise you will not wear a full-length gown with ruffles, bows, or spike heels. Isn't that enough?"

I couldn't bring myself to tell her about my fear of horses with those two girls looking and listening to our every word.

"Yes, but I need to know how authentic this Western wedding will be? You know that even though I grew up on a farm in Maine, I don't do wilderness camping; I am more of a Glamping kinda girl!"

"OMG! Maye, is it the night on the prairie? That is all arranged to make it easy on us dudes, but it is entirely voluntary! Maye, you do not have to go; there are plenty of things to do at the ranch. If you want to stay at the ranch, you can. Are we good now?" She looked at me with such a pitiful look, and I knew my goose was cooked! I would agree with anything!

Relaxing in my chair, I said, "Yes. Thanks for letting me know you won't be disappointed if I stay in my rocking chair on my porch while you ride out into the western twilight."

She looked at me with those big blue eyes, now starting to tear up, and said, "Maye, I would never try to make you do anything you don't want to do; I love you like a Mother or Big Sister!" Those eyes were my downfall; I always gave in when she looked at me like that, and she knew it.

The rest of our spa day went like old times; we were both relaxed, and my body felt good after the facial and massage. She told me about the house Mitch and Al rented, and we laughed ourselves silly over Martha's antics. We love her to death, but she is a piece of work! Seeing people's facial expressions when they first meet her is always fun.

Al and Mich rented office space in a business complex in Metro Center.

Lavonne decorated it in a few days, pleasing Mich by duplicating my office's homey feel. The rental house Martha found for them was around the corner from Nate and Naomi. It was complete with Lavonne-approved furnishings down to the linens and dinnerware.

I stopped by to see their house. Mich and Al were preparing a heavenly-smelling dinner. They were sorry I had to decline the invitation to eat with them. Frank and I were moving in with Mi and Josh and would have dinner with them.

"Maye, let me show you through the house. Martha did a great job finding this house close to Nate. Lavonne did a wonderful job adding a few touches to make it home. She researched the garden for us and put us in touch with a professional. In a few months, we will have mounds of salad fixin's ready for all our friends and us." She was so excited as she showed me all the features of her home and Lavonne's extra touches.

I left to meet Frank at Mi's house and our first night as a couple. I was feeling a little strange but in a good way.

Placing a call to Mi, I asked, "Mi, what do you want me to pick up for dinner; I can stop by Butches and get whatever you want."

"Maye, don't worry. We have dinner planned."

"Mi, we are staying with you, but don't go to a lot of trouble."

"You know we have to eat, too! So get yourself out here so we can enjoy this fabulous meal my sweet husband is preparing."

"Okay, on my way!"

I called Frank as soon as I hung up with Mi and learned he had had the same conversation with Mi. We booked for Lake Haverly. The daily commute would be long for Frank; I would work from Mi's most of the time and only go in for a closing or urgent business. I have to admit, I was looking forward to a little quiet time.

Frank was waiting and hopped out of his patrol car and opened and closed the gate behind us. The view from the hill overlooking Lake Haverly is heavenly; we paused to enjoy the beauty. I have always loved the beautiful tall trees. No matter the drought conditions in Arizona, the area around the lake is still green and beautiful.

The locals believe the lake was connected to the Pacific Ocean in the distant past. They are convinced that there are denizens of the past lurking in its depths. Mi and Josh have plans for future exploration and are experienced divers.

After hugs and help with our luggage, we were treated to a fabulous meal set on the patio strung with lights.

"We are so happy you took us up on our offer to stay with us until your office and apartment are finished."

"Mi, this is wonderful. You will spoil Frank because you know the only cooking I can do is make reservations! I haven't had the heart to tell Mitch the fantastic kitchen she planned will probably go to waste. Lavonne will probably squeal and tell on me."

"I don't think Mitch will think anything of it; from what she said at the party, Al is the cook in her house, too.

"Frank, now that dinner is over, can we ask how the case is going?" Mi asked with a worried look on her face.

"It has been too quiet since Mary Anne stopped that guy in his tracks at Maye's office. However, I suspect we will see some action soon. But you and Josh do not have to worry since you are not involved in this case."

"Not directly, but James and John are worried about Viv and Lavonne. We are worried about you, too!"

James told us John can't decide whether to talk Lavonne into going to Texas or him to come here until the case is closed." Josh said.

"I can understand his fears; I am glad Maye agreed to stay with you; I was worried about her camping out in that vacant half-finished office. I sometimes get into a case and don't come home for several days," Frank said, glancing at me.

"You guys worry about me too much. My gal, Miranda, is always with me and takes good care of me. I agreed with this arrangement to save your back, big guy." I said, looking at Frank.

He said, "I appreciate your thinking of my back, but I was thinking of the miles of paperwork if the bad guys accosted you in that tiny office. Let's not talk about the case, but try to enjoy each other's company for now. If there is anything new, I promise I will share it with you."

Chapter 9 Where in the world is Wanda?

The next day, Frank arrived at his office to find Ward Stone waiting with two Starbucks coffee cups.

"Frank, this is a peace offering. I brought Nate in for an interview; he is on ice, waiting for us. I know he is a client of Maye's, so don't hate the messenger; I am just doing my job. I presumed you would like to set in on the interview?"

"No worries, I have been thinking along those lines too. I would like to be there, and I appreciate the heads-up. I wonder if Nate might be connected to this case by more than just the option house purchase?"

"We know there is a connection between Clarence and Nate; we just don't know what. It is a shame; he is a likable kid, and his folks have a reputation for being top-notch in the construction business. Things have quieted down, and for all we know, Clarence has already found Wanda and silenced her! I don't think he has given up, and my gut tells me this is the calm before the storm."

"The Harris's are doing an excellent job for Maye. I am interested in how Nate knows Wanda Poole. If he knows where she is hiding, is he in touch with her, and is she safe?"

"Good point; I got the address from Viv and sent a couple of agents to make sure she is alive and safe. I wish we could know before we chat with Nate."

"I was sure you already found her," Frank said.

"I wish I could live up to your expectations, but my agents are on the way to where we hope she is right now and will hopefully find her safe. Probably, we will know by tomorrow."

"Thanks for the heads up. I will follow you to your office."

"I will wait to interview Nate until you get there," Ward said and bolted out of his chair. Said a hasty goodbye and flashed out the door.

Frank grabbed his coffee and headed out the door with instructions to hold his calls unless it was an emergency. He mused over Ward's hasty exit. His money was on Ward having the information before the end of the day, probably sooner. He wouldn't be surprised to see Wanda Poole arrive in town. Ward was determined and resourceful! It had been a long time since Frank had met a guy he liked and admired as much.

Frank couldn't help being impressed at the FBI building's size at 7th St. and Deer Valley. It encompassed a large part of the one-mile city block. Frank's department was three buildings close together, but he guessed not as much structure under the roof. He was issued a visitor's badge, and Ward showed him around the building. The equipment impressed him more than the size.

They stopped in the break room, and Ward asked if he had lunch. Frank admitted he hadn't, and Ward treated him to a sandwich and drink. He was a little envious that he could have a hot sandwich and a choice of several different juices or sodas. While they ate, Ward gave him a run-down on what they knew about Nate's activities in Phoenix. None of it was a big surprise. He was sure there was a connection between Clarence, Wanda, and Nate.

After lunch, they entered the room to find Nate sitting quietly at a table with his hands folded in front of him.

He smiled and asked, "Do I need a lawyer present?"

"No, you are not being arrested; we just wanted to talk to you about your relationship with Wanda Poole and her ex-husband Clarence?" Ward said.

The look on Nate's face told them that he knew more than he would be willing to give them without careful probing.

"I don't have any relationship with Wanda or her husband." He said, outwardly remaining calm.

"How did you find out that Wanda wanted to sell her house and that Clarence put her in the hospital?"

"She told me."

"How well did you know them?"

"I met Wanda when I did some handyman work at their house."

"How did they happen to call you? What is the name of your company?

"It is Harris Construction, just like my Dad's company. I figured that if I got a job too big for me, he would be willing to send a crew down to help."

"That is a surprise because we couldn't find any advertisements for Harris Construction in any papers here in Phoenix."

"I only advertised in the small free papers and some mail-outs."

"Come on, Nathan, level with me. If you keep snow-balling, I will assume you have something to hide, and we will do a full-scale investigation into your background, including your parents and your wife."

He looked like a kid caught with his hand in the cookie jar. Sighing and deflating, he started talking. "Alright, I will tell you everything I know. Please keep my family out of this. I got caught up in something because I was desperate. When I arrived in town, I had big plans to make it in the construction business, just like my dad. I didn't realize there are a million handymen and construction companies in the valley. Wanda convinced Clarence to hire me to work on their house, and when he realized my circumstances, he offered me some other work. When I got the job at Wanda's house, I was homeless and hadn't eaten in a couple of days. She took pity on me and fed me."

Nate dropped his head in his hands, and when he lifted his head, looking sad, he took a deep breath and continued. "Clarence had me deliver parts to other garages. He told me he removes parts from crashed cars and sells parts to local garages. He wanted to sell them online, but he knew nothing about computers. I have a degree in Computer Science. He promised me a place in his start-up if I set up the computer program for his business. I was to deliver the parts now, and when he was ready, I would be in charge of that business.

"How long did you realize what business he was involved in?"

"I was so hungry and naïve; Wanda finally clued me in. Naomi and I were dating; we met when she gave me a haircut at one of the homeless shelter's programs to help people get jobs. I was staying with Naomi in her little apartment, and after Amanda was born, my priorities changed."

"What can you tell me about their relationship?"

"Wanda is a master mechanic! Man, she can fix anything! Clarence was out of his mind, jealous! He fancied himself to be superior to any woman. He tried to make her feel inferior to him, but she was so good it blew up in his face. The final straw came when her old boss called and begged her to return to work. Clarence tried to put his foot down and say no, but the marriage was over by then."

"What happened to make him beat her so bad?"

"She told him she was moving out and getting a divorce. He went berserk! The only thing that saved her life was her old boss arriving at her house in response to her call. He pulled a gun, and Clarance took off before the cops arrived. I didn't see him beat her, but appeared as a witness, as did her boss and a neighbor lady. He threatened all of us in court. None of us took him seriously except Wanda."

"When did Wanda tell you about his real business?"

"When I visited her in the hospital after Clarence was arrested and waiting to stand trial. His garage was doing chop-shop business and dealing drugs. Damn, I was so stupid; I didn't know I was delivering anything but used car parts! I don't want to miss seeing my Amanda grow up!" He was now starting to tear up.

"Is there anything else you want to tell me? Anything that will help us will be good for you. I have one more question. Did any of the money you used for the down payment come from the drug or chop-shop business?"

"No. I hope this isn't illegal. Wanda gave me almost all of it. See, as soon as the sale goes through, she will get the money back from the sale."

"I see, so she gave away $30,000.00 and will get back $250,000.00. Do you have to pay her back?"

"No, after she met Naomi and Amanda, she wanted to make sure they would be okay if I had to go to jail. She anticipated you would find out about my part in Clarence's business. Neither of us ever thought that he was capable of murder! I am so sorry." He put his head in his hands and sobbed for several minutes.

"Nate, this will be written, and you will sign it. We will try to keep you out of jail and push for lenience in light of your cooperation. When we find Wanda, will she corroborate your story?"

"God, I hope so! Can I get bail? I want to continue working and be with my family?"

"I don't know; I will do what I can to help you," Ward said.

"Thanks."

We left and waited in Ward's office for the signed confession. Ward made several calls and did what he could to help Nate. He would have to spend a night in jail, but Ward kept him at his facility and out of the general population.

Frank left to head home, probably to eat another fabulous home-cooked meal. Frank and I enjoyed the meals with Josh and Mi, but we were glad we would only stay for two weeks! Our waistlines would suffer if we stayed much longer. We loved full-course type meals for special occasions, not every day.

"Maye, I am already missing your hot tub and am looking forward to the workout bench and treadmill Lavonne is adding." Frank confided privately.

"I miss the hot tub too! We can live without one for a couple weeks, can't we?"

"You know, Hon, you can come to the gym at the precinct and work out and use the hot tub. I can probably arrange to join you. If I can find my suit, did you find yours?"

"No, I don't know where it is. It used to be hanging somewhere by the tub.

"Wait a minute! Frank, do you have a jacuzzi at work? I will look for a suit in town tomorrow. Want me to pick up one for you, too?

Frank said, "Okay, but don't get me one of those Speedo's! He decided not to share with Maye that Ward had questioned Nate and was holding him overnight.

The next morning, they ate as light breakfast as was possible. Josh prepared enough for a dozen people. They each went their separate ways, Maye to shop for suits and Frank to wait for Ward's call.

As it turned out, he didn't have long to wait; Ward arrived before Frank took a bite of his Danish but didn't bring coffee this time.

"Frank, my detectives had a local police officer go with them to the address we had for Wanda Poole, and she hasn't been living there for months! I think she decided she would be safer if no one knew where she was."

"That is not good news."

"I agree, but hopefully, if we can't find her, Clarence can't either, and she is safe for now. I have agents making inquiries to find out where she went. We thought about putting her in protective custody here in Phoenix, but that might make her more accessible to Clarence. And dammit, she isn't the one that should be in jail!" Frank detected the stress in Ward's voice.

"I agree; we don't know how many people Clarence has on his payroll. We'd be stretching our resources, but it has to be her decision; protective custody is no fun."

"I released Nate this morning and am not bringing him in for questioning again until we verify the connection between Nate,

Wanda, and Clarence. I like to know the answers to all the questions I will ask a suspect."

"Yes, I know. Maye told me she could tell that you already knew the answers to the questions you asked her and needed confirmation."

"I read her right, too. The minute I hung up from making the appointment, she was on the phone confirming with my office that I was a legitimate FBI Agent. She had them fax over a copy of my ID and a picture. Most people are intimidated and tell me everything without checking."

"She is a 'take no prisoners' kind of gal! She has told me about some of her encounters with Real Estate agents in her career. She allowed them to think they had the upper hand, and they were always surprised that she held the winning cards." Frank couldn't keep the pride out of his voice.

"I got that impression," Ward said, smiling. "When I find out where Wanda is, I will head out of town to talk to her. Want to come along?"

"Hell, yes!"

"Good, pack a bag and be ready to leave at a minute's notice. Wanda's life may depend on us finding her before Clarence's men."

"I will be ready, and thanks for including me."

They shook hands, and Ward left, not surprised that Frank agreed to come with him.

Frank waited until we were alone to tell me why he was packing a bag. He told me Ward knew Nate had been living on the street and how Naomi helped him. Several scenarios had been tumbling around in my head. I was sure Nate knew Wanda and Clarence. How else could he know about the house? When Nate came to my open house, he made a deal with Wanda and had keys. Agents could (and some would) write a contract around the mortgage and make a quick buck and take a chance on getting sued when the house was forclosed. I wondered how he knew that wasn't a good idea.

The next morning, over a second cup of coffee, Frank's cell rang. From his side of the conversation, I knew it was Ward, and Frank was leaving town. He maneuvered around the questions about the call and the bag by the front door, saying he was replacing his spare uniform at work. A quick kiss, and he sprinted out the door.

I headed out right behind Frank after receiving a call from Mary Anne. She needed me to defuse a situation with clients. The Johnsons were nervous first-time homebuyers. We scheduled the final walk-through on their brand new house in a new development south of Phoenix. I decided to take Mary Anne with me to gain more insight into Real Estate.

Johnson's two adorable little girls were thrilled to have their rooms. We walked room to room, pointing out things that needed repairing. Notes on blue masking tape were placed on the walls. We finished our walk-through, and Mrs. Johnson called the girls downstairs from their future bedrooms. She gasped, seeing them covered head to toe in blue tape. After we got control of ourselves, the rep assured them he would take care of everything. I think they agreed just to get out of there.

The builder knew I would be at the final walk-through with my eagle eye.

Many builders don't like Agents because we advise our clients of things they prefered to skim over. This guy was one of the good ones.

I decided to take Mary Anne to Butch's for one of my Crab and champagne lunches. Butch was thrilled and treated us like royalty ushering us to our table in one of the semi-private alcoves.

"Maye, this is everything you described and more! Butch is a kick in the pants! I don't get hit on often; he made me feel special. Thank you for including me."

Butch returned with a bucket of champagne and sat with us. I was glad he brought three glasses because if the two of us finished a whole bottle, we would need to call a taxi, and might anyway. We laughed and flirted for at least two hours and had so much fun we hated leaving.

MaryAnne was so in love with Butch's that she would become a regular. The food at Butch's is delicious, but he makes the experience delightful.

After several cups of strong coffee, I dropped Mary Anne off at her house and drove back to the lake. After I greeted Mi and Josh, I walked down to the boat ramp. I sat like a kid, with my feet dangling in the water. My mind wandered to Frank and Ward. I hoped they were successful and Wanda was safe.

Frank and Ward headed out of town with intentions to put over half of the 1066 miles to Dallas on the first day, and they did well. They took turns driving, resting, and eating from the cooler filled to the brim with fruit and sandwiches. They decided to stop at a seedy-looking motel not far off I-20 outside of Abilene, Texas.

Snarfing take-out Burgers in the room, they took quick showers and crashed on lumpy beds.

They grabbed a quick Mac breakfast sandwich, gassed the SUV, and headed for Sulfur Springs north of Dallas. Their destination was one of John Kinny's largest ranch customers. Arriving before noon, they were met at the gate by an armed guard looking like a Texas Ranger. Hank Davidson gave them a ranch map and sent them on their way with a friendly wave and a big Texas smile. They were in awe of the size of Hanford Ranch. They knew it was over 500 acres, but until they drove to where John was working, they didn't realize what 'wide open spaces' meant!

John greeted them with man-hugs as they hopped down from Ward's official SUV and invited them into his office in the barn. Offering coffee or ice water, they readily accepted the water, and each gulped down a full glass.

"Thanks, we ran out of water an hour ago and didn't want to take time to stop for refills," Ward said.

"I carry several gallons of water and a cooler of ice when I travel. You could wait a long time beside the road for someone to spot you, and the cell coverage is a little spotty in the country. I have a satellite phone because being delayed could mean life or death to a sick or injured animal."

"We should have known better; we are from the high desert and know water is a priority. We were lead to believe Wanda Poole is working on this ranch." Ward said.

"She did work here for several months but up and left last week! She is an excellent mechanic; any ranch would be lucky to have her. I don't know why she left so suddenly, and before you ask, there is no forwarding address!"

"Did she say anything to give you the impression she was scared or worried?"

"No, she just gave her notice to the owner and packed up and left the next day."

"She was living here on the ranch. Can we look at her room?"

"Sure, we haven't hired a new mechanic, so her rooms are just as she left them. I don't think you will find much; she kept to herself. I gave her a list of other ranches that might be looking for a mechanic. She said thanks, but I don't think she went to any of them. I can check with them; it will only take a few minutes."

Ward and Frank were shown to Wanda's rooms in the barn and searched every square inch. Ward found several receipts, took pictures with his phone, and transferred them to his computer.

John invited them to stay for the night and had lunch delivered.

They gratefully accepted his hospitality.

"The owner is checking his records and asking around to see if anyone heard Wanda talk about where she might be going. He is putting together a list and directions to several ranches that are looking to hire a mechanic. He has several pictures of her and her car. He will send it down with dinner for us tonight."

"Is everyone this hospitable in Texas?" Ward asked, the astonishment showing on his face.

"Yep!" John replied with a big grin. "How is Lavonne doing? I miss her so much; it hurts, but I hope she is having fun."

"She is busy with decorating and having the time of her life planning your wedding. By the way, she and Maye had a spa day. Maye finally admitted that she is more of a Glamper than a camper gal. Lavonne said Maye could go on the camp-out trip or stay in a rocking chair at the ranch. That relaxed Maye so much that she was looking forward to the trip. Lavonne won't show her the dress she will be wearing, and she is a little worried about that." Frank laughed.

"You can tell Maye; it will be a nice flattering dress. She loves Maye and would never do anything to embarrass her."

"In her heart, she knows that, but she still remembers the spike heel episode."

"Tell her I promise I will convince Lavonne to be nice to her feet. Do you guys want to rest before dinner; grab your bags; I will show you to your rooms, and you can settle in for a spell." When the guys saw the accommodations, they kinda wished they could stay longer. The rooms were big enough for a party with King size beds and a bath with a jacuzzi.

After they stashed their bags in the room, they decided a walk was in order and told John they needed to stretch their legs after two days of inactivity.

"No problem, just stay within sight of the Barn and remember our livestock is not fenced or tame. By the way, unless you tell me differently, your steaks will be medium-rare."

They both said, "OK," and wandered off. After seeing a LongHorn up close, they decided to stay within shouting distance of the barn.

After the guys walked for an hour, they returned to their room and spread their work on the desk equipped with a dual-screen computer and printer. Ward attached his laptop to the computer and downloaded his pics of every piece of paper left in Wanda's wastebasket.

They both scanned them for any clues, but she was careful. The only thing they discovered was that Wanda was a pizza addict!

Frank suggested searching for any place in northeast Texas that was looking for a mechanic. They narrowed it down to large ranches but still had a long list.

"Ward, you know she could have gone anywhere and found a job. This will be like looking for a needle in a haystack! I hope the information from Jeb sheds some light on where Wanda may have gone.

"We know she will stay away from big cities and garages that could be connected or unionized. She does have cash; she could be laying on some beach in the Bahamas sipping cocktails while we drive all over Texas."

"Sure enough, but in the meantime, John just texted me that dinner is ready in his digs. I am hungry enough to eat one of those long horns myself!"

They jogged to John's room, and Mr. Hanford himself greeted them.

John introduced them, and he shook hands, saying, "Welcome to Hanford Ranch; if there is anything you need, just let me know. You are welcome to stay as long as you want. Any friend of John's is a friend of mine. I wish I could stay for dinner, but we have a rancher meeting tonight. Here is the information I promised." He handed a large envelope to Ward.

John said, "Thanks, Jeb, for bringing this down yourself. It will be helpful to

Frank and Ward."

"I hope so; Wanda is a fine mechanic, and we hated to lose her. She kept the farm and household vehicles in perfect working order. When you find her, tell her she has a job here, forever." He said.

He spoke to John aside and strode out the door, and they were not surprised to see him mount a huge stallion and ride off at a gallop.

"Well, now that business is handled, let's go into the dining room; dinner is waiting."

They were in awe, seeing Chef George prepare a perfectly fried T-bone steak dinner and a dessert of fresh strawberry Shortcake.

They thanked Chef George profusely for the fantastic dinner and waddled back to their rooms. Both decided to try out the beds and, in minutes, were snoring quietly. Frank woke up in the wee hours and saw Ward at the desk studying the papers from the envelope. He got up and splashed water on his face before joining Ward in reviewing the information.

Picking up several of the pictures thoughtfully included by Jeb, he whistled at the picture of Wanda and her car. "This should make it a little easier to narrow down! A female mechanic driving a powder blue 1949 Rocket 88 with a high compression overhead valve V8 in an Oldsmobile body! Not many will have seen a beauty like this." He tossed it to Ward, heard the whistle from him, and remarked, "The thing that worries me is that Clarence also has the same information; we need to work faster."

"Ward, did you notice what Jeb said about Wanda? She liked hunting with him and the boys, and she is a crack shot."

"Yes, I did, and I think she will stick with the ranches in rural areas and will fit right in because of her expertise with engines and guns. Our best bet would be to split up the names Jeb gave us and call all of them. We should be able to eliminate most of them by the end of the day tomorrow."

"I was thinking the same thing, and sleeping in a comfortable bed one more night won't be a bad thing. Between her being an attractive woman and her muscle car in cherry condition, she can't help being noticed!"

The next day, they called every one of the ranchers on the list, Jeb supplied. They branched out to many of the small towns in northeast Texas with no luck!

"We should talk to Jeb and see if there is an association of ranchers we can get your hands on; it will make our job easier."

That night, they were invited to dinner at the main house. Ward and Frank half expected it to be an estate but were surprised to see a large ranch house instead. They assumed it was modest by Texas standards.

Jeb's wife, Evelyn, met them at the door and walked with them to the living room. She suggested they have a seat and asked if they would like a drink. Conveying their orders to her bartender, she left to check on dinner after making sure the men were comfortable.'

Jeb asked, "Is there anything I can do to help with your search for Wanda?

"Well, now that you mention it, I was wondering if there is a Ranchers Association that lists all of the ranches in Texas?"

"Yes, there is, but you gents should know there are a lot of ranches big and small in this state."

"We assumed there was. We need to find Wanda before her ex-husband does. She is in danger! He threatened to kill her and anyone who helped her! That puts some of our friends in danger, too."

"I am so sorry; why is she in danger from an ex-husband? I figured she was hiding from someone, and I am relieved that I guessed right and she isn't a fugitive."

"No, she isn't a fugitive from the law. Her ex-husband beat her so badly that she sold her house and left town. Only a lawyer and an escrow officer knew the address of where she was hiding."

Frank said nothing, letting Ward take the lead.

"What can I do to help you, boys?"

Ward chose his words carefully. "Is there a way to send word to all of the ranches? Asking for help finding her without alarming her and making her run again?"

Jeb sat back and rubbed his chin, thinking for several minutes. "I have an idea! There are several branches of our Cattlemen's Association.

After dinner, my manager and I will put our heads together, and by morning, I might be able to help you narrow your search down."

Jeb's wife announced, "Dinner is served!"

Jeb escorted his wife, with Ward, Frank, and John following. The dinner was a Prime Rib Roast carved perfectly by Chef George. Later Ward and Frank vowed never to tell Maye or Butch it was the best they ever had.

Chapter 10 Wanda is found.

After dinner, the guys were seated in the living room with after-dinner drinks and enjoying a lively conversation. Jeb had excused himself to meet with his Manager to narrow their search.

He was gone for an hour, returning with a sheaf of papers. "My Manager did some fancy finger work on his computer, and he thinks he can narrow your search to 5 or 6 places. If he is lucky, he will know exactly where she works." Jeb was so pleased with himself that he was almost bursting.

"Jeb, we can't tell you how much we appreciate your help. We will forever be in your debt! Frank nodded his agreement.

Ward and Frank learned that Hanford Ranch is nearly self-contained; they grow most of their food. Jeb employs over a hundred people to maintain a garden and livestock for his private use. He pays them well, and their houses are as roomy and comfortable as the rooms Ward and Frank occupied.

They asked about anyone new coming to the farm that might have spooked Wanda. Jeb said, not to his recollection.

"I remember a salesman who seemed overly curious about what I considered personal stuff. At the time, I thought he was just nosy, but later, when Wanda asked me about him, I recalled he made me uncomfortable. Unfortunately, I can't remember his name, and I threw away his card and brochures. Sorry, I wish I could remember more about him." Evelyn said.

They thanked her but knew if it were one of Clarence's men, the card and brochure would be fake, as would be his name.

Frank and Ward spent some time assuring John that they worked hard to keep

everyone safe at home and had a two-person team following Lavonne.

"John, Lavonne moves pretty fast, but our guys are keeping tabs on her. We haven't told her that she is being watched. Lavonne wouldn't deliberately try to give them the slip if she realized they were following, would she?"

"I don't think so, but I think you should tell her they are there for her protection, and they won't get in the way of her job. I am sure she will co-operate. He said.

"Good to know, you may be right. I will tell the guys to meet with her and let her know it is their job, but they will keep a low profile."

"Thanks, I will sleep better, knowing that you have people protecting her. Well, goodnight, guys. Breakfast will be around 7 AM."

The next morning, they awoke to the cattle's sound; they arrived for breakfast, and Jeb was having coffee with John.

"Good Morning. Did you sleep well? Help yourself to breakfast."

"We slept like babies; everything looks great," Ward said as he loaded his plate and poured a cup of coffee.

Frank followed suit. Their host let them finish their meal before he spoke.

"I have some good news! My manager found Wanda and has been in touch with her! He told her about you coming all this way to make sure she was okay.

"Wow! Your manager worked miracles; thanks a lot! Where is she? We will start immediately to pick her up and head for home." Ward said.

"No need! She was working at a ranch in the central part of Texas. Being a woman mechanic and driving that car made her stand out! The ranch where she worked was willing to post guards to protect her if she stayed, but my manager convinced her she might be better off with you guys. I would pay top dollar for her to come back and work for me. I am afraid we will have a bidding war between us ranchers to see who gets her to stay." He drawled.

John said, "Maybe she can do the mechanic work like I do my Veterinary work; that way, y'all can have her work all the ranches."

"That's a great idea; when she gets here, I will approach her with the idea, but I get her first!" He said with a big Texas grin on his face.

"Jeb, I am grateful for your help, but I am worried about her driving back here alone; maybe we should go pick her up."

"You boys, just relax and enjoy another day or two on the ranch; she will have a convoy of two of my friend's vehicles in front and behind her. She will be safe. I guarantee it! They aren't Federal Marshall's, but they are every bit as capable, and she is capable of protecting herself.! When she got here, she had never held a gun. She is a fast learner and has become a crack-shot!

Frank called Maye as soon as he got to the room after breakfast.

"Hi, Maye. We will be spending several days here at the ranch. Wanda is being escorted to the ranch by several of Jeb's friends, and she should arrive here tomorrow.

"Will it be just you and Ward bringing Wanda home?"

"No, I think that Ward has planned to have several Federal Marshalls escorting us to Phoenix.

"I am looking forward to having my bedmate back!"

"We are being treated royally, but I am having trouble sleeping too. I gotta tell you, Texas hospitality is the bomb!"

"Well, don't get too spoiled; you will have to come back down to reality when you get home. I didn't learn to cook while you were away."

"Ah, but you have other qualities that more than make up for it!"

"Want to hear something funny? Yesterday, a truck delivered a Jacuzzi to Mi and Josh's! I wore my suit, but it was heavenly and has room for four people. Mi said, "You can use it while yours is being held hostage. She and Josh looked pleased as punch when they saw the look on my face. How did we get so lucky to have friends like them?"

"I don't know; maybe it is because you are a wonderful friend. I am lucky I found you, and want to lie beside you in bed for the rest of my life. I love you, Ms. West!"

"I love you, too, Mr. Singleton; I like that idea."

It wasn't in Ward's character to sit and wait for someone else to do his job, but he did try to relax. Several of Jeb's men gave the guys a tour of the ranch, and after a day in the saddle, they were grateful for the spa in the rooms.

The next morning, their discussions centered around what to do with Wanda once she was in Phoenix. They were trying to think of how to protect her without putting her in a jail-like position.

"I think from what I have learned about her, Wanda will balk at protective custody with a guard and be confined to one room in a safe house. What do you think, Ward?"

"My mind is running on the same track as yours. Maybe Wanda will have some ideas of her own since she is tired of running. I have a feeling she will want to settle with Clarence."

"I was thinking the same thing, but I don't think he has changed his mind. I can understand his anger when the marriage soured, but this is more than a marital disagreement. There is more! Wanda has something on him that he doesn't want her to talk about, and he will do anything to keep it quiet!"

"I wonder how deeply Nate is involved?"

"The connection between Nate, Wanda, and Clarence is more than that house! Something infuriated Clarence and split their marriage wide open. I can't imagine finding her sleeping around would cause him to want to kill her. It has to be something else!"

"I think so, too, Ward. It will be good to get home to Maye and our trial marriage! We were trying to keep it under wraps, but the construction has blown that all to hell!" Frank said with a silly grin.

"That's no big deal! You two were made for each other!"

Both guys spent the rest of the day resting in a couple of comfy rockers on the veranda outside their room, enjoying watching the longhorns until they fell asleep.

The sun was setting when John woke them, saying, "Hey, wake up, you guys! It's dinner time, and we have a guest!"

"Are we eating at the main house or in your room?" Ward inquired, yawning.

"We are eating in my room, but Jeb and Evelyn will join us along with our guest."

He would not tell them who was coming for dinner. They roused themselves and decided that a shower was in order and dressed in their best.

Entering John's room, they were surprised to see Wanda Poole! She was a striking woman with her well-proportioned slim frame. Her long, curly wheat-colored hair held at the nape of her neck with a sparkly clip, allowing it to flow over her slender shoulders. She didn't need much makeup to be attractive, and her sheath of dark blue matched her smoldering dark eyes.

Wanda stepped forward and said, "Hello, I am Wanda Poole, although I suspect you already know that! I understand you have been looking for me?" She said. Her smile captured the men's attention; she stepped forward, shaking both men's hands, calling them by name.

"Good to finally meet you, Wanda." They said.

Jeb and Evelyn arrived before anyone could start talking business. "Now that introductions are over, let's eat dinner before it gets cold," Jeb said.

No one needed any prompting. The sizzling steaks on the grill gave the incentive to comply. Chef George outdid himself with huge t-bone steaks, oven-baked potatoes, and fresh broccoli from the garden. He had a sweet strawberry pie for dessert.

After dinner, the group moved to the sitting room to enjoy after-dinner drinks. When everyone was comfortable, Jeb looked over at Wanda. He said, "Wanda, I know these gentlemen are curious why you decided to give up hiding from your husband and come back!"

"I might have stayed out of Clarence's reach forever. But I have realized it would mean never forming relationships with good people. I knew soon after I married him that he had a violent temper. Even after he beat me to a pulp, putting me in the hospital, I didn't think he would commit murder! I am so sorry about people dying because of me. I understand one of his men threatened a woman receptionist at the Real Estate Company. She put one of his thugs in his place! I can't wait to meet her! I cannot stay here safe and protected and allow him to hurt people. It has to stop!"

"Have you been in contact with Clarence in any way while you were hiding? We wondered because you left the safe house several months ago. Did he or one of his men find you?" Ward asked.

"Well, yes and no. A couple of months ago, I started feeling uneasy, like someone was watching me. And once or twice, it felt like stuff in my room had been disturbed. I moved, leaving no forwarding address, but the feeling didn't go away. I decided to come back because I was homesick for the ranch. Jeb and Evelyn have been so good to me that I decided to come back and beg for my job! The ranch owner where I was working told me a couple of cops were looking for me, and Jeb was helping them find me. I respect Jeb, and that made my decision.

"Wanda, you are not responsible for those deaths; men hired by your husband committed them. You had every right to protect yourself! By the way, you did an excellent job of hiding; It would have taken us much longer without Jeb's help. Our job now is to figure out how to keep you safe in Phoenix and how to keep Clarence from wreaking any more havoc on our friends." Ward took the lead, and Frank did not interrupt.

"Wanda, we are glad we found you safe; a lot of people were worried about you. We wish we could tell you that you will be safe when you return to Phoenix, but that is not the case. Clarence has made threats against everyone who helped you with the sale of your house. Many of them are friends of ours."

Frank's phone buzzed, and he said, "Please excuse me. I have to take this call." He got up and walked out to the patio for privacy.

Shirl Packard, his second in command, was on the line. "Boss, I have some disturbing news; last night, James and Viv were ambushed and run off the road by two guys in an SUV. James' truck landed in the ditch on its side, but they got out of the seat belts and returned fire while calling for help. They received minor flesh wounds and were out of ammunition when the bad guys were approaching the truck; sirens scared them off."

"Are they okay? Did they get the license number? Description?"

"No license number, a vague description, it happened so fast. Viv and James were treated and released from the hospital. "

"That's good. Wanda is with us on the ranch where John works, and she has agreed to return with us; we have to figure a way to keep her and everyone else safe."

Shirl took a deep breath and said, Boss, there is something else. You decide whether to keep this from John. Lavonne has disappeared! We told her that she was being watched; she said she was okay and thanked us. She went into David's Bridal Shop to try on wedding dresses. She never came out! We questioned everyone in the shop and searched every square inch of it and the stores for several blocks."

"Son of a bitch! I will get back to you in a few minutes; in the meantime, put every person on it and, for God's sake, keep it from Maye!"

"Will do my best! What is your eta?"

"We will be leaving at first light! And will drive straight through! Until we get on a freeway, it will be spotty for cell service. Thanks for the heads up!"

Frank stood for a few minutes before he went back in. He took a deep breath and steeled himself before telling John his beloved Lavonne was missing.

He paused in the doorway, then motioned to Ward, "Could I have a word?" He closed the door, told Ward everything that happened, and asked, "I need your advice; Lavonne is Maye's best friend and John's fiance. Should I keep the fact that Lavonne is missing from John until we know for sure she is in trouble?"

"No. Tell John now!" We need to catch the next flight out of here."

"I agree." They both returned to the room, dreading telling John.

"Sorry for leaving, but my second in command wanted to fill me in on what is happening in Phoenix. James Crandall and Viv Appleton were ambushed and run off the road; they are okay, only sustained flesh wounds before help arrived. Frank started to tell about Lavonne, but before he could say anything, John had his cell to his ear, screaming. "Where the hell is Lavonne? She always answers, no matter what she is doing. I can tell by the look on your faces you know why she isn't answering!

"John, hold on a minute...

Chapter 11 Lavonne is kidnapped.

Everyone rushed to Frank and Ward, surrounding them and all talking at once. Ward said loud enough to get their attention, "If you will all step back, we will give you the information Frank received from his office."

But John was not going to sit or be quiet; his beloved Lavonne was in trouble, and he knew it! Jeb started talking gently to John until he calmed enough to sit. Resting his hands on John's shoulders, he said, "Okay, boys, give us the information, and we will see how we can help."

Frank took the floor: "James and Viv were wounded when their truck was forced off the road. They are okay, shaken up, but okay. Lavonne was aware of and was okay with the two men we assigned to her. She went into David's Bridal Shop to look for dresses and never came out. Our men and several detectives from Ward's have questioned everyone in the store. So far, we haven't found her."

"John, do you think she may have gone out one of the other doors, not thinking about checking in with the men?"

John jumped up over the objections of Jeb and said, "No, of course not! We have to get Phoenix!" He looked like he was going to leave right then.

Ward said, "John, we will leave right now if you want or first thing in the morning."

Jeb said, "That won't be necessary; I can get you all to Phoenix faster than that! He asked George, "Is the plane ready for a flight tonight?"

"Yes, sir. I can file the flight plan as soon as we get to the airport, and we can be in the air in 20 minutes."

"Evie, Hon, I will drop you at the house. We leave here in 15 minutes!"

Frank and James sprinted to their rooms, packed their bags, and met Wanda with her suitcase, coming out of her old room. They jumped in the back, Jeb sped away, and in what seemed like seconds, he dropped Evie at the house and spun gravel down the road to his private hangar. They were loaded and in the air in 10 minutes.

As soon as they were in the air, and it was quiet, Frank approached the cockpit and asked, "Where are we landing?"

"We are heading for Sky Harbor; I have rented a private hangar."

"I will have my officers meet us and escort us to the station. If that's okay with you."

"Absolutely."

Ward called his office and ordered a team to meet at Frank's office.

John withdrew into himself and didn't acknowledge anyone. The trip to Phoenix seemed to take forever; Frank and Ward were chomping, anxious to check on how Lavonne could or would give their men the slip.

Looking around, they had to admit Jeb knew how to live. They observed that his jet seated six comfortably and had a bedroom and a small kitchenette supplied with smacks and drinks. John was sitting, continually redialing his phone and listening to Lavonne's voice telling him, "Hi John, I love you! I am with a client and can't talk right now; I will call you right back." She had her phone programmed to answer John's number with this message and a generic one for everyone else.

Frank and Ward were coordinating the search for Lavonne. Agents searched the entire shop and interviewed everyone who worked that day. Wanda acted as hostess and kept everyone supplied with drinks. Ward and Frank took black coffee, and Jeb told her John liked cream and a little sugar. She added some Baily's Irish Crème to John's coffee. He appeared to doze off for several minutes, only to suddenly wake up and start dialing. George and Jeb took black coffee. She fixed her coffee like John's and sat to read a book.

It appeared to be smooth sailing, with no storms or wild air currents, and they landed in Sky Harbor with no problem. The rented hangar was on a private airstrip reserved for luxury jets.

Several of his officers were waiting when Frank stepped down and took care of their luggage. George, Jeb, and Wanda, with her arm hooked with a quiet John, were the last to leave the plane. Several agents and officers surrounded them, leading them to the waiting vehicles. Word should not have leaked out about the flight's arrival, but they remained cautious because of Wanda. She seemed to be oblivious to the fact she was now in Phoenix and could be in danger.

The cars drove straight to the back of the Sheriff's building. Guards escorted everyone into the building and to the conference room on the top floor.

John refused offers of snacks and drinks, mumbling, "I don't need or want any damn drinks! I want to know where my Lavonne is?" He had at least stopped shouting.

Jeb put his hand around his shoulder again and said, "Son, these people are working on it. Give them a chance to tell us about their progress."

Shirl and Brenda had everyone's attention, and Shirl stated, "We have talked to everyone that worked at the bridal shop, and they all passed background checks. Every store for several blocks was canvased. The street and security cameras on all the stores for several miles surrounding the store are being checked. There is no sign of Lavonne walking out of the store alone or with anyone else. We checked all the store patrons; so far, if we didn't know better, it would appear that she vanished into thin air. We know that didn't happen! We are focusing on someone taking her out disguised or in a way that didn't arouse suspicion."

"So, you don't know where she is or who took her yet?" Asked Jeb, still sitting next to John.

"We are sorry to say, at this minute, no, we do not. Our officers and FBI are looking at all the security cameras, and we will let you know when we have any news," Brenda added.

John seemed to deflate, sinking into his chair. Jeb sat beside him, keeping his arm around his shoulder, murmuring to him, keeping him calm and quiet.

Ward approached Frank and said, "If a reporter gets in Maye's face with questions, or if she sees it on the news, I wouldn't want to be in your shoes!"

"My God, you are right! I need to find her and tell her right now!"

Frank started for the door, and it swung open, hitting him with such force it knocked him back several paces. He lost his balance and landed on his ass! He saw my angry face, standing with hands on my hips, ready to battle!

"What the hell are all of you doing here? I thought you were in Texas! Who are all these people?" I shouted, looking around the room.

"Maye, I will tell you everything; just take a breath, okay?" He said, getting to his feet and putting his hands up in defense.

"I was leaving the office, and a newspaper reporter accosted me, asking me if I wanted to make a statement about the kidnapping? What God Damned kidnapping? Why would they think I would know about a kidnapping?" I said, finally stopping to take that breath Frank wanted me to take.

Taking my arm, he pulled me to a corner. "Maye, Hon, the gentleman over there with John is Jeb Hanford, and the other man is George, his pilot and chef. The woman is Wanda Poole. We just flew in on Jeb's private jet. Shirl called us last night and said Lavonne went into David's Bridal Shop to look for dresses. Did you go with her? Do you know where she is?"

"No, of course, I didn't go with her! You know very well that she won't even let us see any of the sketches of the clothes we will be wearing. What makes you think she would let me go shopping with her? I said, my anger starting to take a back seat to the fear restricting my breathing, and the picture forming in my mind stunned me into silence.

"Maye, she is not answering her phone. Could she have lost it?"

"What? No way, she takes care of that phone like a baby. There is no way she would misplace it! Oh, My God! Someone took her! Why would anyone do that? It can't be!" By this time, my voice was an agonizing whisper.

He tried to put his arms around me, and I pushed them off so hard they went flying. I stepped back, ready for a fight. "Not Lavonne! Nooo!" I lost myself in the horror of seeing my gentle Lavonne in the hands of kidnappers! Immediately, I saw a vision of sweet Lavonne standing in the middle of the room in her panties, crying while the bad guys laughed at her!

"Damit, Frank!" I was seeing red! "So, what are you doing to find her?" Tears were forming and threatening to fall, which, by the way, is a dangerous time to be near me! If I am angry enough to cry, people should run! Frank is one brave man! He stepped closer and, hesitating a few seconds, folded me into his arms, letting my head rest on his chest.

My first instinct was to shout and scream, but I realized that would not help poor John. I got control of myself and stepped back. Frank led me over and introduced me to Wanda and George. After our introductions, I kneeled and put my arms around John, not saying anything, just hugging and crying with him. I asked, "John, would you like me to take you to your Father's place, or do you want me to have him come here to be with you?"

Jeb said, "I think going out to his house would be better. We can't be of help here, and being with family would be good. By the way, I am Jeb, and it is nice to meet you. Frank has talked a lot about you."

Frank broke into the conversation and said, "I will have a car take you out to James. Jeb said, "No need, I have a car waiting, and it will hold everyone that wants to go. I would like to meet John's Dad."

Jeb said to everyone in the room, "We are taking John to his Father's house. Anyone wanting to come along is welcome."

Wanda said, "If it isn't an imposition, I would like to go too. I don't have family in town, and unless the police need me, I feel safe with you, Jeb."

"No problem. Y'all are welcome at my Dad's house. I'll call him on the way out and warn him how many are invading his home!" John said, a little calmer now that his mind was on his Dad.

I put my arms around Frank and said, "I think I will go with them, and later, someone can take me over to Mi and Josh's house. See you later tonight or tomorrow. We kissed, and I followed everyone out the door.

Chapter 12 A full house.

I sat up front with Jeb to give him directions. Wanda sat in the back with John and George in the middle seat. When we arrived at the gate, George hopped out and opened and closed it behind us.

As we crested the hill, Jeb spotted the American Eagle's nest in the tree. He became excited, "I've got to get a couple of close-ups of those eagles!"

"Take all the pictures you want, but don't attempt to climb up for a better view; the owners of this property do not want them disturbed."

"Lord have mercy, I would never try something so crude; I have some pretty good telephoto lens. When I get the perfect shot, I will have it enlarged and framed for Evie. She will love it."

"Take the left; you will go by two houses on this road; our destination is the last house."

"There are only three homes on this lake?"

"There are four; the property owner, including the houses, lives across from the eagle nest."

"Nice! I would love to meet them and ask permission to set up my camera on their property."

"They are friends of mine, and I will be happy to introduce you."

"Thank you, kindly; I appreciate it."

"The house should be around the next corner. There it is, and James and Viv are waiting for us. The construction is coming along, and there will be plenty of room with the new addition."

The minute they stopped, Viv and James bounded down the steps, holding

John tightly for several minutes. He said, "Thanks, Dad, for putting us all up."

"No problem, we have plenty of room. We now have four bedrooms and 2 ½ baths. We only have finishing left to do. Come on in, everybody; we have coffee, tea, and sandwiches."

As soon as they entered the kitchen, John introduced Jeb, George, and Wanda to everyone. If Viv and James were surprised to see Wanda, they didn't show it. They greeted everyone and invited them to eat.

We sat around the table, chatting like old friends, watchful of what we said, not wanting to send John off the deep end. He contributed little to our conversation, only answering questions.

James showed us through the house, and when he took us out to the back porch with the magnificent view of the lake, Jeb and George were ready to get out on the lake and fish. They were disappointed that Frank suggested no one go out on the lake until the danger passed. They reluctantly came inside, only to gravitate to the porch later to watch the sunset. Jeb took dozens of pictures of the magnificent colors. He even got several clear shots of the eagles flying out for their evening hunt.

His smile looked like he had won the lottery when he reviewed his images.

He exclaimed, "Evie will love these and insist I bring her back to visit."

James said, "It will be our pleasure to have you and your wife as our guests."

"That is very generous of you, and I gratefully accept. I can't wait to get the chance to do some fishing. We can book accommodations in town."

"You will do no such thing! We have plenty of room, and it is a long ride from town." Viv interrupted.

"Ma'am, thank you. I appreciate the chance to get on that lake and fish, and bagging a Javelina would be fun. I love to hunt, too, but I like the security of a rifle."

"I like the rifle too! The guys like hunting with their crossbows, and James is pretty fast with his and is teaching Josh and John."

"Well, Viv, we will have to go along to protect these men with their little bows and arrows!"

Viv laughed and said, "It is a date!"

"Viv won't touch the crossbow, but she is every bit as good with a rifle," James said.

"John has been planning on teaching me, and if I could get as fast as James, I would love to try my hand at a real quarry," Jeb said.

"Does Evie hunt?"

"No, she will target practice and loves skeet shooting but is too soft-hearted to kill an animal. But if she were in danger, she would do the job and cry later." His pride showed on his face. George peeked out the door and said, "Dinner is ready."

Their noses were assailed with the aroma of real Italian Marinara sauce. They saw the smiling face of George behind a large dish of sauce and spaghetti on the kitchen table and the smell of fresh garlic bread. George was as tall as James, with a full head of white wavy hair setting off his blue eyes. James opened two bottles of Red wine and poured as soon as everyone was seated.

Wanda encouraged John to have a plate by telling him, "You need to keep your strength up. Lavonne will need you when she gets home."

That perked him up a little, and he managed to eat a small plate and was encouraged to have wine. Wanda kept his glass full, and by the time he had finished his second glass, he was relaxed. His eyelids were closing, and he could barely hold his head up.

James and Viv gently led him to his room and put him to bed. They walked arm in arm back to the party, anxious to learn everything from Jeb and Wanda now, without hurting John.

Now that we couldn't hurt John by talking freely. We kept our voices low and listened to James and Viv tell about their harrowing experience on the road home last night.

"We were starving and picked up a Papa Murphy's pizza for dinner. I couldn't wait to get home and pop it in the oven. You know I have been taking Viv to work, staying in town, and driving her home every day. We were on the last turn to our house when, from out of nowhere, we were rammed on the driver's side so hard I lost control and veered off the road and landed in the ditch."

Viv took up the narrative, saying, "I slipped out of my seatbelt while James was struggling with his and got my gun out of my purse. I peeked over the side of the truck to see two ugly guys coming across the road with automatics. I think they expected us to be injured and not able to return fire; I'm pretty sure I hit the first guy, slowing down their assault."

James jumped in, continuing, "By that time, I got out of the seat belt and got my gun. Viv had them running for cover instead of advancing on us. Between the two of us, we held them off. The cop cars arrived just in time; we were out of ammunition! Our wounds were only in the fleshy part of our arms, really just scratches; the Doctor said a chest or stomach wound would be a different story; we would be in the hospital or dead.

"I think those guys were surprised we were able to return fire. From now on, I will have rifles and plenty of ammunition in my truck! We think Viv winged one of them seriously enough that he will need medical attention. There was a good-sized blood trail to their vehicle. Frank is checking on that. But in the meantime, that is our story; if you want to share your story, we are all ears?"

They looked so proud of themselves that we all clapped and cheered quietly so as not to wake John.

I hugged Viv and said, "I am so sorry I brought that deal to you; I never thought it was anything but a lease option! If I had any idea that there would be any danger, especially to my friends, I would never have written it."

She and James hugged me from each side and said, "Maye, we know you would never do anything to hurt your friends. You couldn't know there would be this kind of trouble writing a contract. We aren't sorry to be a part of helping a nice guy like Nate."

Looking nervous, Wanda said, "I hope you feel the same way about me after I tell you my story. I know I will have to repeat it to the cops, but I want you all to know how much I appreciate you taking me in without knowing if I was involved in Clarence's dealings. First, let me put your fears at rest! I never participated in the illegal part of his business. My big mistake was to marry the jerk!"

"He allowed me to work because I was better than his mechanics. He would never let me near the books. But, as time went on, I learned what he didn't want me to know. I knew he had to be doing something illegal! His shop couldn't support our lifestyle. I found his real money-makers were loan-sharking chop-shopping, and he had something on several high-profile people. He was being 'helped' by them to avoid the law. They had no choice in finding him guilty of assault. I was still in the hospital when he was sentenced. I was disappointed in the short prison sentence, only 10 years.

"Maye, Viv, I owe you big time for putting that sale together with Nate. It gave me time to heal mentally and physically. I saw an ad in a magazine for a mechanic on a Texas farm and decided to apply. It was great living on the ranch." She said, smiling at Jeb.

"Clarence was pissed that I didn't recant like the other women and let him off the hook! But what the cops don't know yet is I stole a couple of his ledgers detailing his business, with names and dates! I think he decided that if I was dead, I could not turn them over to the cops! If someone hadn't called the cops, he would have succeeded. He must have panicked to learn I survived."

"Are the books hidden here in Phoenix?"

"Yes, they are, Jeb! I would never put you and Evie in danger! Clarence knows they are in Phoenix! I had a lot of time to think in the hospital and discovered the perfect hiding place! It should give you a good laugh. Clarence won't laugh, though, and he will be more dangerous when he finds out I am here in Phoenix and ready to talk to the police. He will go nuts!"

"Oh, My God! He may already know you are back in town! He must know Lavonne is my best friend? He will use her as leverage to force us to pressure you into giving up the books!

"Maye, didn't you recently interview several agents who wanted to come on board at your office?" Viv asked.

"Yes, Frank and Ward are vetting them, but they have been so busy I am afraid it is on the back burner. I have had potential agents visit the office several times to get a sense of how they will fit in with Sarah, Michael, and George. They had to see Lavonne flitting in and out with her wedding books. Dammit! I should have been more careful!"

"Wanda, if it becomes necessary to exchange the books for Lavonne, will you agree to it?"

"Absolutely, I was planning on turning them over to the police, anyway. How could I refuse? Just an FYI, I digitized the whole thing before I hid the books, and I have them right here on this keyring!" She said slyly, holding up a replica of her 88 Rocket car. She laughed out loud and was delighted to hear everyone join in the laughter.

"Frank and Ward can check on the validity of copies of the books vs. the paper version; maybe we can give the books in exchange for Lavonne and still have the upper hand."

"Before they are exchanged, it will be necessary to be sure the copies will fly in court! But it is good to know we can exchange them if needed." Jeb asserted.

Viv asked, "More wine, anyone?" She was getting another bottle when they heard a car drive in the yard. Everyone except Jeb and Wanda brandished guns pointed at the door.

Everyone breathed a sigh of relief when they heard Frank's voice saying, "Put the guns away; it's only me!"

He walked in and immediately took me in his arms, hugging me for several minutes. Looking over my shoulder, he said, "Have you got more of that wine? I would love a glass."

Within minutes, Viv had a glass in front of him, and James poured for everyone again. Frank took a long drink and sat, looking down at his glass for several minutes. "I was hoping to go home and get a few hours of sleep and a change of clothes. But I can tell from the look on your faces that's not going to happen until I tell you what's happening."

"We really are worried about John and Lavonne. We put John to bed several hours ago and have been catching up. Wanda also has some news for you, but that can wait." I said.

As I talked, he emptied his glass, and Viv filled it again. Sitting up straight, he looked at us with tired, sad eyes. I could see that what he was going to tell us was hurting him, too. "We thought Lavonne was wheeled out of the shop in a trash can. But the store manager confirmed there was no trash pick up scheduled for today." Before he could continue, I exploded, "How dare those bastards put Lavonne in a trash bucket! They are going to pay dearly for that!"

Everyone shushed me so I wouldn't wake John, but I continued to fume inside.

"We confirmed it was a diversion to keep us busy while they got her out a different way. Ward figured it out! He counted every person coming into the shop and leaving, and he didn't discover a discrepancy in the numbers. The numbers added up! He noticed two gentlemen entered the shop separately but left with another man walking between them. They were walking almost arm in arm, and the man in the middle was much smaller and shorter, which aroused his suspicion. Maye, you will love this; the small man in the middle tipped his head up briefly and winked at the camera in front of the building!"

Holding his hands to stop the questions, he said, "She took a big chance dropping her little lacy hanky on the ground and pulling a long piece of hair down in the back! She is one brave and smart young lady!"

By now, my tears and Viv's were threatening, and our hands clasped without us being aware. The guys were sitting on the edge of their seats in rapt attention. Wanda faded into the background and silently filled her glass again.

"We got closeup pictures of both men's faces, and our IT guy enhanced them as much as possible. We put a bolo on them, with the stipulation not to apprehend!"

"What?" Four voices said.

"We want to follow them in hopes they lead us to where they are holding Lavonne. If we arrest them, their lawyers will spring them before we talk to them. Our officers are instructed to find them and only transmit to us where they are and their vehicles' make, model, and license number. When I left, they hadn't finished running the pictures through Ward's database." He pulled two pictures out of his pocket and handed them to Wanda. She appeared at his side when he mentioned pictures.

"Wanda, take a good look. Do you recognize either of these men?" She studied them for several minutes and then handed them back.

"No, I am sorry, they look familiar, but I can't put a name to the face. Do you have another set? I want to study them; I promise to call immediately if I remember anything."

"No problem, that set is for you," He said, handing them back to her.

"Thanks, maybe the name will come to me. I didn't meet all of Clarence's men. Frank, I have some additional information for you, but by the looks of your face, I think it can wait until morning." She got nods from all heads.

Frank said, "Thanks; I need to get a little sleep and go back to the office."

We said our goodnights and left for some much-needed rest, at least we hoped. When we pulled up to Mi and Josh's house, the lights were on in the kitchen and living room, and the minute we walked in the door, we were assailed with questions.

Frank gave them an edited version of the events of the last few days. They did not interrupt him to their credit, and when he was done, they hugged us and ushered us to bed. We did not argue, and in minutes of throwing off our clothes and climbing into bed, we were both sound asleep.

Chapter 13 Video and Revelations.

We slept a little later than we meant to, and Frank was hot to get to the office. After a quick shower, he gulped down the scrambled eggs, kissed me goodbye, and scooted out the door.

After he left, Mi, Josh, and I had a more leisurely breakfast. Over coffee, Mi wondered aloud if Wanda would reveal the book's hiding place and if the police had to surrender them to get Lavonne back safe and sound.

"If they have to give up the original books, will the copies fly in Arizona law? I asked.

"You would need solid proof that they are in Clarence's handwriting to admit them as evidence. Clarence could still maintain no knowledge of them. I do more corporate than criminal law, but the evidentiary rules are often parallel. I would have to do some research to give a definite answer."

"Thanks, Mi. Would you do that? I am sure Frank and Ward have legal counsel, but they probably won't tell me anything. Lavonne has to get home safe! She is my little sister and the daughter I never had! I will do anything to protect her and have no problem taking the law into my own hands!" I said, fear and anger engulfing my body.

Mi and Josh made a case of letting the law take care of it and not getting myself or Frank into trouble. I pretended to calm my exterior and agree with them, hoping they were satisfied.

As soon as I could extricate myself from the loving and protective arms of Mi and Josh, I drove to the office. I needed to concentrate on anything except Lavonne's situation! My apartment and the addition were finished except for the trim. The Hot Tub and exercise area were still open to prying eyes, but I needed to move in. We could sneak out in the dark to use the hot tub. The front office was finished, and MaryAnne was ensconced at her desk. The agent's offices in the added building were still under construction.

I picked up the phone to ask Lavonne how soon the beds would arrive, and my heart ached when I remembered I couldn't ask her anything! A cloud of depression enveloped me, and I put my head down on my desk and sobbed quietly. After a good cry, I cleaned myself up, admonishing myself for doubting Frank. He would get my Lavonne back! He had grown to love her as much as me.

Leaning back in my brand new comfy chair, I was grateful Lavonne insisted on adding. I had to almost slap myself to keep from falling asleep.

My computer beeped, telling me I had an email. I hurriedly opened it and was greeted with a recorded message from Frank. "Maye, Honey, I am sorry I can't be with you when you see this, but MaryAnne should be knocking on your door any second to view it with you. Please try not to worry. Every available agent is working on this video; however, if you or Mary Anne see anything to give us an idea of where she is, call immediately." And sure enough, Mary Anne knocked and came in, pulling up a chair beside me, not acknowledging my blotchy face.

I opened the video and unplugged my headset so Mary Anne could hear. I gasped when I saw Lavonne primly sitting in a chair, still wearing the suit she wore when she was taken from the shop. I sat up straight, my eyes glued to the screen. She read from a prepared script: "Hi Maye, don't worry, I am being treated very well. The four men have promised to drop me off at your office when you deliver the books Wanda Poole has in her possession. I have a comfortable room with a view of"…She was cut off mid-sentence. When the video resumed, her smile didn't fool me for a minute. It was evident that she was told to not talk about her surroundings. "Oops, sorry, I forgot why I am talking to you, Maye. Anyway, don't worry about me; I am being treated well. They treated me to some great take-out. Maye, it is so good we have to go there for lunch. I think it will become our favorite place to eat." She was interrupted again, and the film had a blank space for several seconds.

When she started talking, one cheek was a little red! Red-hot fury engulfed me, and MaryAnne put her hand on mine to calm me.

She looked up at someone appearing to be standing close to her and said, "Sorry, I forgot myself; it won't happen again." Looking into the camera, she said," Maye, don't be mad at me. I know you want John and me to have a big formal wedding. I think we might just catch a flight to Las Vegas and elope! I promise, when we get back, you can throw a big reception in the library at Mi's house."

Looking up at someone out of the picture with those big blue eyes, she asked sweetly, "Can I tell her what you gave me for dinner? It might ease her mind a little? Maye, we had Crab and Cheddar on English muffins. You have to try it! I know you will love it. It has become my favorite, and I hope to have it again." She gushed, and before they cut off the video, she winked at me with a big smile and said, "Love you."

The video ended; they left a picture of Lavonne sitting in a chair with that sweet smile. The gruff male voice said, "Miss West, we know Miss Lavonne Hall is your best friend! Now, we don't want anything to happen to her, do we? So here is what you are gonna do. You will convince Wanda Poole to give you the package she stole from Clarence. You have 24 hours. We will call with instructions, and you will follow them to the letter! When we have the package, we will return your little friend, unharmed, to your office. We know you are in contact with the cops, and one is your boyfriend! But we warn you, if we even smell cops near the drop-off site, all bets are off, and your little friend will be the one to suffer."

For several minutes, Mary Anne and I sat in stunned silence. The phone ringing jumped us into life. It was from Frank. "Maye, did you or Mary Anne get anything from the tape? We think she was trying to tell us she is near the airport, and they are getting take-out from Butches. Did you get anything else?"

"I wish I did, but I think all the rest was just fluff to cover up those two things." Mary Anne agreed with me but said she would study it to see if she could get anything else. I planned on doing that, too! I would have the crew at James' house have a look, also. Frank was way ahead of me and had sent a copy to them. He said, "We got an invitation to dinner at James, and I accepted, hoping it would be okay with you. Mi and Josh will be there; why don't you bring Mary Anne?"

Frank, "I don't think a dinner party is appropriate when Lavonne is in danger."

"Maye, it isn't a party; we need to make sure Wanda can lay her hands on those books and find out if anyone else gleaned anything from that tape. I don't like the setup, but it is what it is. Maye, I promise you, I will get Lavonne back." *"Great, now I have to worry about him too!*

Mary Anne decided that she didn't need to be the fifth wheel on the wagon and would instead go home and study the video, promising to call if she came up with any clues. I popped into my office bath and attempted to erase the effects of the afternoon crying jag. Not totally satisfied with the results, I tucked my computer in my attache case with my headset. I hurried to my van and sped out of town as fast as I could during the start of the evening commuter traffic.

The video repeatedly played in my mind during the long drive to James. I was hoping something Lavonne said about the room would jump out and give me a clue about where she was.

When I arrived at the gate, I saw Jeb's car on the other side. George opened the gate. I drove up beside Jeb's van and rolled down the window.

"You guys leaving town? Is everything okay?"

"Shucks, no, we aren't leaving. Everything is just fine. We are heading into Punkin Center or Prescott to pick up supplies."

"Thank you for being so helpful; it means a lot!"

"That's what neighbors do!" Jeb said with his big Texas grin.

I drove through, and George shut the gate behind them, and they took off spinning gravel. When Mi added the 2 bedrooms to James' house, she enlarged the parking area, which now accommodated 6 or more vehicles. I parked so I could hopefully make a quick exit without inconveniencing anyone.

Coming through the door, the tantalizing smell of something cooking assaulted my nose, and my stomach growled in protest of being denied food all day.

Viv had just opened a new bottle of wine and poured me a glass. I asked for a snack, and Viv quickly cut cheese, adding crackers, grabbed the bottle, and led me to the back porch. We sat side by side, enjoying our snacks and the relaxing view.

"Dinner will be around 7:00. Will this hold you until then?"

"I think so."

"None of us had much of an appetite today. John has been in a zombie state since he watched the video. We couldn't stop him from looking at it over and over. James suggested that John help him discourage the Javalina'a from getting close to their home. It was the first time John smiled a little, but he insisted on taking the satellite phone if there was news. James is hoping it will keep John busy until dinner."

"Viv, I must have looked at that video a hundred times this afternoon and got nothing!"

"Maye, I have been looking at the video, too, and I think I know what Lavonne was trying to tell us. I think she isn't far from the Bridal shop, which is a couple miles from the airport! Remember she said you wanted a big formal wedding? Well, we know that isn't true! You would like a small informal wedding. And she said she and John might fly to Vegas and skip the big wedding? We know that her first husband talked her into eloping, and that turned out badly. I remembered you telling me she almost died the first time they had sex."

I broke in, saying, "OMG! You don't think they are raping her, do you?" Horror showing on my face.

"Hold on, Maye, that isn't what I was saying at all! I think she told us that she is near the airport and David's Bridal or close to another bridal shop near the airport. I think she wants us to look for those men in sex traffickers' files; they may have a record in that area. And, before you ask, I already talked to Frank, and he gave Ward the heads up to check it out."

Breathing again, feeling a tiny sigh of relief, I took her hand and said, "Viv, thanks for the heads up, and good work. Every time I looked at the video this afternoon, all I could see was those big, scared eyes. I don't think I can stand it if anything happens to her."

Viv put her arms around me, hugged me for several minutes, and said, "Maye, if you need a good cry, I will hold you as long as you need. You aren't just my colleague but my best friend, too!"

"Thanks, Viv; I thought my eyes would give me away. I had a good cry this afternoon!"

"Nope, you look beautiful! Just sit back and look at the scenery; I'll be right back with a small sandwich and another bottle of wine."

She disappeared and returned in a flash with a sandwich, which we split, and enjoyed another glass of wine, waiting for the guys to get back from town.

Frank, in the meantime, was having a different experience. His office and conference room were a beehive of activity. It was filled with people talking and putting pictures and notes in black, marking pen on whiteboards, and several IT guys rapidly tapping on keyboards and printers spewing papers. People were sorting, stapling, or adding pages to the whiteboard.

When Ward stepped into the room, the noise level didn't cease but lowered a few decibels. They shook hands, and Ward, seeing the anxious look on Frank's face, pulled him aside.

"I took your advice and ran those faces through the sex-traffic database and got a couple of hits!" Ward quickly added, "The two men are low-level in the business, which is good for us because when we apprehend them, they will roll on anyone above them. We know or are pretty sure, given the other facts, that the trail will lead us back to Clarence Poole. Putting him away for a long time will make me a happy man."

"Me too, Ward, but I am not sure how that will help us get Lavonne back. She is my priority right now. Maye and John are barely holding it together, and I don't know if they will make it if Lavonne is hurt or worse! I remember Maye's reaction when Lavonne was humiliated!

I agree! We have to find them before Maye gets to them, or we will have a ton of paperwork to submit!" And his slight grin softened Frank's somber mood a little.

"Yeah, and we should remember John, Jeb, and George are Texans and might be more inclined to take the law into their own hands. I hope we have enough men to watch them and the bad guys!" Both grinned, but it looked more like grimaces.

"Ward, I know there is a lot of work that I could and should do here, but I need to see how Maye and John are holding up. My main priority is to get my hands on those books! I won't hesitate to give them up to get Lavonne released unharmed! Getting a conviction for kidnapping is okay, but putting Clarence away for the things in those books would be the icing on the cake." Frank said.

"Don't worry, we can hold down the fort here. Go ahead, but call me the minute you have possession of those books! By the way, let me know when and where you and Wanda will go to get them, and I will be there to back you up. I would appreciate that when you get your hands on that drive, copy it, and send it to me."

"Good idea; it will give Maye and Viv something to keep their minds occupied."

Ward said, "Since we think they are getting take-out from Butches, we have supplied him with pictures of two guys we know about. I have a couple guys watching the surveillance cameras in stores, on the streets around the airport, and Butch's. The minute we spot them, we will have several officers on them."

He continued, "My officers haven't reported seeing the two guys that took Lavonne out of the shop on the streets, which tells me they are lying low, knowing we saw their ugly faces. The guys holding Lavonne will be getting hungry soon, and with any luck, they will go back to Butch's, and we can follow them back to their hideout. We have agents watching all the places around the airport. We had the city set their cameras to take pictures of every person that sets foot in and out the door of every take-out restaurant within ten city blocks of the airport! We are putting several people on the feed from the cameras to get them viewed fast!"

"Ward, we appreciate having your team working with us. I can't thank you enough!!"

"Go on and get out of here."

Frank hoped to have a few seconds with Maye before he was inundated with questions. It seemed to be ten times further to the lake, and he hadn't slept in 48 hours, and he was beat! The strong take-out coffee only partially did the trick, and when he finally drove into James's yard, he sat for several seconds with his head resting on the wheel.

Taking a deep breath, he got out and walked to the door. Before he could give his usual knock and "Don't shoot!" greeting, he was met by James and John coming back from their hunting trip. John had a knapsack that looked stuffed with a small game, and James had a large bag on his back that looked suspiciously like a small Javelina inside. John said, "I look forward to what Chef George will fix with this fresh game. I got several rabbits, and Dad got a small Javelina!" Frank was cheered, seeing John's slight smile.

He needn't have worried about getting in the door; no one was paying any attention, knowing officers were stationed in the yard. He thought, "*I need to warn them to be vigilant and not to depend on the officers.*"

As they entered the kitchen, they greeted George and were assailed by something smelling delicious. The aroma made their stomachs growl so loud they sounded like wild animals.

"Hello, George, how soon is dinner? I am starving!" Frank said and was followed by James and John's questioning looks.

"It is ready right now! It is one of my family's Goulash recipes, but I have added a few things, and now we call it Jeb's Texas Goulash! If you call everyone to dinner, we can eat right now."

George handed Frank a huge bowl, and he started eating. George placed the pot full of Goulash on a hot plate in the center of the table, along with two platters of fresh hot biscuits.

In minutes, the table was filled with hungry appetites, and shortly, the bowl was empty, as were both plates of biscuits. John ate a little, but he was consumed with worry over Lavonne. He allowed Frank time to eat before he asked, "Frank, what is happening? I need to know how soon my Lavonne will be at home."

Chapter 14 Why me?

"Maye is right; a big purse is a sign of an undisciplined mind! I need my appointment and sketchbook, and I'll be darned if they aren't missing. Now, where are you hiding?" Murmured, an exasperated Lavonne, her face nearly buried in her bag, pawing like a dog, "Oh, there you are! Okay, I need to see Angelique about the bridesmaids' dresses and shoes. They should have a formal western flair and the color, hmm..."

"Mademoiselle Hall, I am Angelique, " a husky accented voice said behind Lavonne, startling her out of her reverie. Spinning around, she lost her balance, and two strong arms prevented her from falling. They were attached to an attractive woman looking down, her makeup flawlessly applied, giving her the appearance of a much younger woman than her actual years.

Lavonne smiled, showing her adorable dimples, noticing Angelique's dress had simple, clean lines with little adornment. Maye might pick one like it for herself, but Maye would never dream of painting her face to the extent of Angelique. Maye claimed she had no talent for applying makeup or hairstyling, but Lavonne thought Maye looked great. She wore very little makeup, and her red hair had just enough natural curl to fall into place with a light brushing after a shower.

"Hello, Mademoiselle Angelique; thank you for making time for me today. I am planning a June wedding at a Dude Ranch in northwest Arizona and am looking for formal attire with a Western flair. My Mother of the Bride's dress must be stylish and comfortable. She would say she has been my best friend for a hundred years, but we have known each other for closer to 15 years in reality. The one thing she abhors is buttons, bows, ruffles, and spike heels! By the way, she would love a dress similar to yours.

"Merci beaucoup! Would Mademoiselle like to share your sketches for creating your outfits, or would you like to select from our one-of-a-kind dresses? Have you selected your color scheme? Will your wedding be outdoors or in a chapel? Are you thinking of authentic Western styles?"

"Please call me Lavonne, Angelique, and right now, I am thinking of having the ceremony in the quaint chapel on the grounds. We probably won't have snow, but it could rain in June in northwest Arizona. Blue is my favorite color; I would like to see some of your dresses and compare them to my sketches."

Angelique clapped her hands and said aloud, "Dresses in shades of blue with a Western flair." She spoke into a small mike concealed on her collar.

Lavonne was oblivious to everything except people coming and going. She only had eyes for the dresses she was shown and picked several for later consideration. When Angelique asked if she would like to try on one of her own wedding dress designs, Lavonne squealed with delight!

She was led to a spacious changing room decorated all in white with a floor-to-ceiling mirror. An attendant instructed her to remove her outerwear as she unzipped the full vinyl bag. Lavonne turned her back to the attendant, and before she could unbutton her blouse, she heard a noise like "Umph," and spinning around, she saw the attendant slump to the floor. Two men appeared from nowhere and stepped close to her, one pointing a huge gun at her, saying, "Don't scream, and we won't hurt you."

With saucer eyes, she gulped, "I don't have much money with me, but here, take it all!" She said, holding her bag out to the biggest man close to her.

"We don't want yer money, honey! Do as I tell you and be quick about it! Put these clothes on over yours. We are going to take a little trip, and if we get what we want, we will send you back home to your friend, Maye West, real soon!" He said, patting the big gun he tucked in his belt.

She was so stunned she stood like a statue for several minutes. The biggest guy put his hand on his gun, still in his belt, and said, "Move!" Loud enough to shake her out of her frozen state.

She stuttered, "Oh, Okay, d d don't shoot!

He threw a sack on the couch and said, "Hurry up and get dressed in these clothes."

Lavonne fumbled with the men's zippers and buttons but managed to get the alien clothes on her body.

He handed her a wide-brimmed hat and said, "Put this on and hide all that messy hair."

She sniffed as she said, "Messy hair, indeed! Can I please have one of my hankies? I think I'm coming down with a cold." The man fished in her handbag and handed her one of her dainty hankies, saying, "Okay, girly, let's get outta here!" She sniffed loudly, saying, "Thank you very much." Looking up at him, she smiled, showing him her beautiful eyes and dimples. The minute his back was turned, she pulled a small bit of hair down from the back, so it fell down over the collar of her coat.

The two guys, one on each side, marched her out of the dressing room and out the back door.

Lavonne noticed the street camera. Looking up briefly, smiled and winked. She deftly dropped her hanky at the corner. Her kidnappers were nervously looking from side to side as they pushed her into the back of the car. She was surprised they didn't blindfold her immediately. After a couple blocks, the guy in the back with her pulled out a black cloth bag and shoved it over her head. Damn, she tried to concentrate on how many turns they made, but she lost count after a while and heard planes landing and taking off.

Lavonne was walked into a building, up a flight of stairs, and pushed into a room. The door slammed shut behind her, and she heard the click of a lock. She pulled off the sack and was dismayed at the shabby bed, lounge chair, and a tilted table and chair. She opened the only door, revealing an even shabbier bathroom without a window! She left the awful clothes and hat on the floor, happy she had been allowed to put them on over her own clothes.

Slumping down on the lumpy bed, she pushed herself into the corner, pulling her knees up to her chest and hugging them with her slim arms. She held back the tears of frustration forming in her eyes, trying to figure out why she was kidnapped! *"I don't understand! I don't have any money; John makes a good living, but not enough to warrant a ransom! Maye also does well, but she isn't wealthy either! There must be something else they want. Oh, my poor John and Maye; they must be so scared and angry! Oh dear, I wouldn't want to be one of those guys if they hurt me or worse. Maye is deadly when she is angry!"* She allowed herself a nervous giggle, remembering the housewarming. John grew up as a real Texan; between them, they make a make a no-prisoners pair! She knew that seeing her kidnapper's faces was not a good sign, and her promise not to tell would be ignored.

A little later, the door opened; a plate of food and several water bottles were deposited on the tiny table. It delighted her to see the lettering on the bag was from Butches. *"Well, at least they are feeding me well!"* She was sure she was near the airport and Butches. She had to think of a way to hint that she was near both. She paced the floor until exhausted, settled on the bed, and fell asleep. When she woke up, she fixed her hair and makeup. If John saw her looking beautiful, he wouldn't be so scared. She sketched the men's faces in her datebook.

Chapter 15 Hiding in Plain Sight

The minute dinner was over, John started questioning Frank about where Lavonne was being held. He said, "John, I won't lie to you; we don't know where Lavonne is right now, but we are following every lead. When you looked at the video, did you get any clues?"

"No, I've looked at it a million times and got nothing! I just can't think!" He said, running his fingers through his hair. He added, "Viv watched it, and she figured out that she is somewhere near the airport and Butch's. Maybe they will go there for more food, and you can follow them!"

The hopeful look on his face tore Frank up, and he said. "John, why don't you look at it again and try to listen for sounds other than airplanes? It could be significant."

"Okay, Frank, I will." John took his phone, found a quiet place, added earbuds, and became oblivious to everyone.

I motioned Frank to follow me, and James handed us beer when we stepped on the porch. After a long swallow, Frank gave them the rundown on what was being done and what they hoped to accomplish. Finishing with, "I need to get my hands on those books." He said, looking at Wanda.

"Is it okay if I take you to them in the morning? We will need some tools to get them out of my hiding place. We left Texas in such a hurry I didn't have time to grab my mechanic tools. I think you will appreciate where they are hiding in plain sight! She said with a satisfied grin on her face.

"What exactly do you mean, hiding in plain sight?" If they are in plain sight, why hasn't Clarence found them?" Frank asked.

Clarence is not a Master Mechanic! That was always a sore point between us! A mere woman being a Master Mechanic just wasn't palatable!"

She held up her key ring and said, "You all thought my little car was the right hiding place for the drive, but the vehicle where I hid the book is under Clarence's nose. I can't wait to see the look on his face when I tell him where they have been all this time." It looked like she was having fun, and Frank hated ending her enjoyment, but he needed those books!

"Wanda, I am sorry to spoil your fun, but we need to know where the books are now! Please give the drive to Maye and Viv? They will send a copy to Ward so he can check with his legal department to determine if it can be used in court to convict Clarence."

"Sorry, it has been such a long time since I have been on the up-side of this battle; I just wanted to enjoy it a bit longer." She said, looking chagrinned.

Frank laid a map on the table for her to point out the location.

She laughed and said, "A map won't be necessary; we only have to drive to the corner of 7th Ave and Northern. The Oldsmobile Dealership has stood on that corner for 50 years. The owner, Frederick Furgeson, and I were friends long before I met Clarence. I worked for him for years and still have keys to his garage."

"I'll call Ward and arrange to retrieve them before Clarence gets wind of where they are... But before he could dial his cell, she put her hand on his arm to stop him.

"Wait, you will need the rest of my information and my help unless you or Ward are Master Mechanics and can get your hands on a crane!"

With a confused and slightly angry he said, "Look, Wanda, no more fooling around. We don't have time for games; where the hell are those books?" This isn't rocket science; why can't we go get them?"

She grinned, "It's interesting you use the term rocket science! That is exactly what it is: rocket without the science!"

Frank's patience was starting to wear thin; he said, "Okay, spit it out! Exactly where are those damn books!

"Sorry, Frank, but that dealership covers the whole city block, and they not only sell new and used Oldsmobiles but do restoration work on vintage cars. That is where I used to work. As a matter of fact, when I found my little Rocket 88, Fred let me use his garage to do the restoration on my baby."

"OMG! You didn't hide it in your car; that is in Texas!" Jeb broke in.

"No, I would never do anything to put you and Evie in danger!. The books are in the car's engine, mounted on top of the dealership. It is a twin to my working model, and she is shrouded in a transparent resin coffin! The coffin might be opened, and someone with my knowledge could get to the books, but not without damaging the car's engine. And I won't let that happen! I insist on being the one to take the engine apart. After extracting the books, I will put her back together carefully. She is a classic, and we intend she remains that way forever!"

Jeb interjected, "Wait a minute, the books are inside the car's engine, parked on a dealership roof in the middle of the city? How in hell can you take the engine apart in broad daylight? You will be seen by hundreds of people? Someone will tell Clarence and the jig will be up!"

Frank was stunned hearing the narrative of where the books were and imagining the nightmare of retrieving them. "*If Clarence's men beat us to the punch, Lavonne's life won't be worth a nickel.*"

The silence was deafening, and Wanda couldn't stand it; she blurted out, "I don't understand your fears. I will have no problem getting books. We can leave now if you have the tools I need."

James said, "I did most of the mechanic work on my old truck and have a pretty good supply of tools. You are welcome to use them."

"Cool, show them to me, and I will tell you if you have enough and what I will need," Wanda said.

Jeb was puzzled by her explanation, "It will be obvious that something is going on when people see a crew of people on the roof!

Taking the coffin off the roof intact, you would require a crane, which would be visible for blocks."

"Why would we need a crane?" Obviously, you don't know much about car dealerships. I can bring the crate down from the roof with the same lift we used to get it up there!"

"Hot dam, woman, the owner was in on your plans! Jeb said, admiration showing in his voice.

"Yes, he worked out how to get the box on the roof and how to take it down from inside the dealership. He originally planned on putting a different car in the box every few weeks. But when he visited me in the hospital, he suggested this alternative. Its mechanics are pretty unique, but I will let him tell you all about it if that is okay with you? He hasn't been able to brag about it and deserves bragging rights."

"How soon can we go get them?"

"The dealership is open from 8 am to 8pm every day. I can call Fred and set it up for around 8:30 tonight; that will give him plenty of time to get all the customers and salespeople out the door."

"All right, call Mr. Furgeson and alert him of our arrival. Make sure he understands that there will be quite a few cop cars arriving."

Wanda headed out to the porch to make her call, and Frank called Ward and told him where the books were hidden. Ward couldn't help being impressed with Wanda's ingenuity, especially when he learned the car was on the roof in plain sight. Ward said he would meet him at the dealership at 8:30.

Wanda came in at about the same time Frank hung up. She said, "It's all set.

Fred will be waiting for us at 8:30. I won't need any tools; Fred has an identical set to mine that I left in Texas!"

At precisely 8:30, Ward's crew arrived in two black SUVs and were stationed among the lot cars. Frank, Jeb, George, and Wanda drove in and immediately went to the showroom. Brenda and Shirl pulled in last and parked close to the entrance.

James convinced John that Lavonne would be mad at him if he got hurt. I was enlisted to stay and help James and Viv keep an eye on John and keep him from leaving the house. Frank didn't fool me a bit; he wanted to keep me safe and avoid the paperwork if I used my weapon.

Fred Furgeson opened the showroom door and ushered them inside. Wanda threw her arms around Fred; they hugged. Pulling apart, Wanda said, "Guys, this is Fred Furgeson, my best friend!" Fred stood about three inches taller than Wanda and had a shock of white curly hair, piercing brown eyes, and a neatly trimmed mustache and goatee. He obviously visited the gym regularly and looked comfortable with the gun strapped to his waist.

He said, "Wanda, girl, what have you gotten yourself into?" Showing a slight Irish brogue.

"Nothing like the last mess you helped me out of, Fred! Do you remember when we put that twin of my Rocket 88 up on the roof? Well, tonight, we will take it down and retrieve a set of books I hid in the engine. They are important to these nice folks to convict Clarence of more than just beating me up!"

"Just beating you up, you say? Girl, it's a miracle you are alive after what that monster did to you. I stepped in just in time, or he would have killed you!"

"Maybe so, but right now, we need to get those books because a nice young
lady has been kidnapped by some of Clarence's men. Her price of freedom is those books. So, will you show my friends how to get the car down and help me take the engine apart?"

"No problem, it will be my pleasure! Follow me! He said.

Wanda halted him before he could start walking to the back of the building. "Fred, before we get knee-deep in that engine, I'd like to introduce you to some people who have been helping me!" She introduced Ward, Frank, Jeb, and George. Fred shook everyone's hands, saying, "Good to meet you. Any friend of Wanda's is a friend of mine."

Jeb said, "George and I will stay out front and look over all these lovely new cars."

"Guess we'd better get to it!" Fred said as he started walking briskly to the back of the dealership, next to the service department. He opened a panel on the wall and pulled a lever. Hearing the sound of something being rolled across the roof, instantly the crew looked up,

Wanda slipped away from the group and disappeared., leaving Fred time to do some bragging.

"We solved the part of getting the car up there and taking it down without disturbing my showroom. It is pulled up from this area by a ramp and moved from the back to the front on tracks with a hydraulic pulley system."

"When this building was under construction, we planned a two-story building, but extra land became available, so we expanded out instead of up for the time being. This left us with more than adequate structural roof strength to allow the car, the tracks, and the mechanism. We built a ramp like the ones in parking garages to drive a car up to the roof and back down. Wanda wouldn't allow her baby's twin to be in the open air of Phoenix, even for a day! Our compromise was the resin box! We put it on wheels to make it easier to roll down the ramp."

"Why didn't you just drive it up to the box?" Ward said.

"Wanda wouldn't let us drive it, even that far! It has never had oil or

gasoline inside since it was put together! It is for show only! Many of the parts in the car had to be hand-tooled because they were no longer available. Wanda built them herself by hand."

He hardly finished that sentence when they heard the motor's screeching! Its progress was halted, but it continued to struggle to move forward.

All eyes were looking up, and Fred said, "Oh! Oh! I think we hit a snag! Someone will have to go up on the roof and free the mechanism. That will cause a short delay." He opened the door again and pushed a button. A square outline on the ceiling became an opening, and a ladder slid down to the floor.

Wanda returned, wearing well-worn coveralls with the letters WP in sequins, saying, "Fred, better shut everything down so no one loses a hand!"

She put her foot on the bottom, rung of the ladder, and bounded up to the ceiling. Frank and Ward headed up behind her, and before they got close, she had unlatched the top opening, pushed it open, and stepped out on the roof. By the time the guys reached the top, she was halfway to the box.

"Go back and tell Fred to send up tools. We need to dig a mess of debris out of the tracks. Frank hollered Wanda's instructions down to Fred.

In a few minutes, Fred climbed out of the hole with a satchel bulging with tools. He jogged to them and set the bag on the roof, opening it so Wanda could pick out the tools she wanted. She started handing tools to the men, "As soon as we get these tracks cleaned, we can move the box over to the large square, back there." She pointed to a place about 20 feet in the back of the building. When she was satisfied that the tracks were clear, she asked the guys to climb down, and she would stay behind and follow the box down. They started down the ladder, but Ward held back, saying, "I am staying with you, just in case!"

"In case of what? No one knew we were coming here, and anyone would assume that Fred is just changing the car."

"Clarence knows you used to work for Fred. I am sure that Clarence has spies looking for any unusual activity. This would qualify, don't you think? If I were a betting man, I would bet he not only knows you are in town but where you are staying."

"But how could he know that? No one knew I was coming back to Arizona, and I only told Fred about wanting to get the books late this afternoon!"

"Think about the timing of Maye's friend being kidnapped. Don't you think it was a little too convenient? It was right after you decided to come out of hiding."

"Now that you mention it, yes, it is a big coincidence!"

"If I am right, we had better get the hell off this roof ASAP! We are sitting ducks!"

Ward called down to Frank, "Better have eyes on the front of the lot. I have a funny feeling we are going to have company."

Wanda quickly closed the trap door, and they walked briskly to where the box would settle before being lowered to the floor.

As they walked, they could hear the sound of the gears coming to life, and the box followed them to the square spot on the roof where it stopped.

Securely hooking links to the box, she said, "Ward, have Fred start the mechanism to allow the box with the car to slowly roll down the circular ramp to the next level.

Ward made the call, looking in all directions, seeing a helicopter in the distance, and asked Frank to check on it. The square squealed open, and one end of the box lowered slowly until it was at a 45-degree angle and slowly rolled off, starting the descent to the floor below. They stared transfixed, watching the box slide out of sight. Ward suggested that Wanda climb down the ladder, and he would wait until the box was on the ground and walk down the ramp.

Wanda started for the ladder. Ward's phone rang, and at the same time, several bullets slammed into the rooftop, way too close for comfort! Ward was sure the helicopter was the culprit, but he couldn't hear the blades. He sprinted to Wanda, knocking her to the roof, covering her with his body, saying, "When I roll off you, head for the door, and I will cover you!"

"Hell, you will, get the fuck off me, so I can get my gun out! Our best bet is to make it to the ramp now!" Ward realized she was right, and they crawled as fast as they could toward the ramp. At the same time, trying to see which direction the shots came from. They were almost to the ramp when Wanda rolled over and fired several shots over Ward's head. He looked back and saw a man fall from the roof several buildings from them."

They scrambled off the roof and down the ramp several feet. Ward scrambled to his feet and started running down the ramp. He came to a screeching halt when he realized he wasn't hearing footsteps behind him.

He ran up the ramp and saw Wanda pulling her scarf off her neck and wrapping it around her thigh. By the time he reached her, the scarf was bright red with her blood! He tightened the scarf enough to stop the blood flow.

She said, "No worries, it's just a flesh wound, not close to the bone. It wasn't from a high-powered rifle, or I would be in big trouble. Help me up so we can get downstairs! They will need our help!"

"Can you walk?" Ward asked.

"Yes, I can." He put his arm around her, helping her to a standing position; she put her arm over his shoulder."

Ward thought, "*I could stay up here and return fire, but my pistol is no match for their automatics, and no matter how tough Wanda thinks she is, she needs medical attention!.*"

When they reached the floor, they saw several of the big front windows were shattered, and cars had multiple bullet holes in them.

Frank was swearing, "Dammit, the rifles are in the van!"

Seeing Wanda's leg, he said, "Put her in one of the offices and come help!"

"The hell you will! This is my fight, and this is just a flesh wound!"

Ward scooted her behind a car and said, "Listen, you stay down! You can't go fast enough not to be an easy target, and we need you to get those books!"

She nodded her agreement and stayed low behind the car.

"Use the vehicles in the showroom for cover!" Fred called, "No worries, I have insurance!" He scooted over to Wanda as soon as he could.

They looked up in horror as a large SUV came crashing through the smashed window, screeching to a stop and sliding around so the back was toward them. "Don't shoot; we brought guns!" Brenda hollered through an open window as she returned fire to someone on the roof across the road.

"Frank and Ward ran low to the back of the van; as they got near the back, the door opened, and Brenda and Shirl jumped out. Unlocking the rear hatch, they handed rifles and clips to them. Ducking behind vehicles, they took rifles to the guys in the showroom.

Wanda, Fred, Jeb, and George gave them cover, and now all four were armed with rifles. The shooters on the ground started approaching the smashed window, thinking they would overcome them with superior weaponry. They had plenty of cover as the lot was full to capacity for a weekend sale. The minute the shooters realized the people in the building had equal firepower, they retreated, and the shots ceased.

Frank, Ward, Brenda, and Shirl scouted for several blocks around the dealership but saw no shooters. They returned to the building, taking up positions and keeping an eye on the parking lot.

Wanda and Fred headed back to the box to check on her car. "Girl, you need to go to the hospital; I can get your books," Fred said.

"Not going to happen! I am staying right here until I finish the job, but your help will be appreciated." She said, wincing as she pulled herself up and put her arm over his shoulder.

"I sure hope those books do the trick and that little lady is freed unharmed. Your friends are determined to get her back and keep custody of the books! I sure hope they pull it off, but I have my doubts." Fred confided to Wanda as they made their way to the box.

"If it can be done, those two guys will do it! They traveled to East Texas to find me before Clarence's men could shut me up. Their friends have taken me in, fed me, and given me clothes. I kinda left in a hurry. I would love to use those books to put Clarence away forever, but poor John is a Zombie without his Lavonne, and right at this moment, she is my main focus."

Fred had changed into his work overalls and rolled out his toolbox as she leaned against the wall. He produced a key from his pocket and unlocked the box. He jumped back laughing as all four walls fell with a crash to the floor and bounced a couple times. The noise brought Ward and Frank, guns drawn, running to the back, saying, "Are you guys alright?"

They stood breathless, watching Fred and Wanda laugh! "You could have let us in on the joke; you scared us half to death!"

"Sorry, no more crashes, we promise," Fred said.

Ward saw that Wanda's wound was seeping blood. There was a good-sized red pool where she had been leaning against the wall. She ignored it. They were engrossed in opening the hood of the car. Wanda unhooked it from its mooring, and they lifted it off to make it easier to hoist the engine out of the compartment. Attaching carefully padded lines, Fred started the hoist. He carefully swung the engine over to a metal table. Setting it down delicately, he connected padded straps to hold it securely.

Wanda seemed to be oblivious to pain or the blood seeping from her wound. Fred worried that Wanda was going into shock and continued watching her. He would call a halt to her participation in dismantling the car if he felt she was in trouble. In the next hour, she and Fred worked steadily until they had carefully dismantled the block, and Wanda reached in and pulled out the books. She held them high in the air, giving a stilted victory dance. Fred would have joined her, but seeing how white her face had become, he put his arm firmly around her waist. Wanda and Fred walked out front to deliver the books to Ward and Frank.

Chapter 16 Waiting for the call.

The officers were standing around the snack bar with cups of coffee and munching donuts, seemingly unfazed that minutes before, they were fighting for their lives. Frank and Ward had already called in a preliminary report to their bosses and then to Maye and Candy.

Wanda, propped up by Fred's arm around her, held out the books. She wondered if there would be a fight over who got custody. Frank took the books, laid them on the bench, and placed a call for an ambulance. Wanda put her hand on his arm and said, "Frank, this is just a scratch; I don't need an ambulance. I need a clean bandage, a shower, and a good night's sleep. Besides, don't we have a Doctor at James'house?"

Frank put his phone away and asked Fred, "You know her better than we do. Does she need to go to the hospital?"

"It would be a good idea, but you are right; I do know her better than you. She is as stubborn as a mule, and she will fight you every step of the way. Let the Doctor look at it and argue with her. It looks like the bleeding has almost stopped."

Wanda was emboldened by winning the ambulance war! She was determined to stay and help Fred put the engine back together. Wanda was fading, even if she didn't know it. She argued, "This was my baby! Fred, you know I hand-tooled most of the parts to this car, and I intend to stay here and put her back together!" Standing unsteadily with both fists planted on her hips.

Ward and Frank vetoed that, threatening to put her in protective custody until the exchange. Ward tightened the scarf around her leg, picked her up over her protest, and placed her in Frank's car. Fred put his hands on her shoulders, leaning in nose-to-nose, and said, "Wanda Girl, I promise I will lock up your engine, and it will be waiting for you to put it back together, yourself. Your job will be waiting for you when you are ready!

They were hoping for time enough to look over the books before they had to give them up, but there was no question of whether they would give them up for the safe return of John's beloved Lavonne. Ward left three officers to guard Fred.

Frank carried Wanda into the house over her objections. Viv placed a folded sheet on the couch and told Frank to lay her down. She started to loosen the scarf to look at the wound. "Frank, why the hell didn't you take her to the hospital? This isn't just a scratch! She needs medical attention!"

"She flatly refused!" Frank said.

"Dammit! Get out of my way! I need bandages and lots of alcohol." James started for the bedroom to get the needed items.

Hearing the heated exchange of words and the sight of Wanda's leg brought John out of his fog, and he insisted on looking at it. He hollered to James to bring his bag. Wanda, pale and dazed, had no fight left! John cut her pant leg off and cleaned and dressed the wound. He said, "This can only be considered a flesh wound by a long stretch of the imagination! Wanda, you lost a lot of blood! This is a temporary bandage, and I am giving you a shot of antibiotics! You will be okay tonight, but I insist you are taken to the ER tomorrow for an x-ray to make sure there aren't any bullet or bone fragments!" He gave her a shot that would allow her some relief from the pain, assuring her it wouldn't knock her out.

"Thanks, John. I appreciate the help, but I really would like a shower as soon as I get my sea legs! Viv, sorry for ruining your pants."

Viv said, "Damn, those pants were my favorites, too." Wanda looked like she was about to cry when Viv laughed, saying, "Come on, let's get you in the shower and some clean clothes." She helped Wanda to her feet and, with James's help, to their bedroom. She found clean clothes and turned on the shower.

"Do you need some help? If you feel dizzy, I can wait or shower with you." Viv said to Wanda,

"No, thanks. I appreciate the offer, but I've been hurt a lot worse than this.

Go back out and hear about the guy's bravery. When I come out, please have a stiff drink waiting."

Viv said as she went out the door, "You got it, girl!"

George was whipping up some delicious side dishes for dinner. The Javalina was on the bar-be-cue being turned by an electric motor. The smell of the Javalina on the grill and bread baking was intoxicating.

Viv and I had drifted to the porch to enjoy listening to Jeb and George tell their exciting tale of the shoot-out at the car dealership.

I asked Viv if Wanda would be okay, and she said, "Yes, it really is a flesh wound, and it was good to see John take charge, and he seemed enthused about the exciting book retrieval. I'm sure he thinks his Lavonne will be with him soon."

We both hoped he was right. Viv confided to me. "You know, Maye, I will be sorry to see George and Jeb head back to Texas. We are looking forward to when Jeb brings Evie back for a visit. Selfishly, we hope Chef George will be their pilot. Maye, we are so spoiled! James and I need some Gym work and several good runs to work off the extra pounds."

"I know what you mean! I can't wait to move back to my own apartment and my hot tub and exercise spa. I will need to swim ten miles a day to work off the rich food we have been treated to every night and the magnificent breakfasts cooked by Josh every morning."

"Did you look over the copies of the books Frank had us send to him and Ward?"

"I did a quick skim read, and I can see why Clarence wants them back. He had his hands in many pies and had dirt on several leaders in the community. I'm not surprised that he is desperate enough to shoot up a big dealership in the center of Phoenix."

"We should be hearing from the kidnappers about the exchange. It would be perfect if the feds could free Lavonne without giving up the books.

"That would be sweet, but this is real life, and that only happens in the movies."

Wanda appeared on the back porch, gently easing herself into the chair, and downed the drink in one swallow, saying, "Thanks, I needed that!"

Viv said, "Yes, you did! Do you need another?"

"No, the smell of that Javalina is tantalizing, and I want to be awake to enjoy it. Viv, Maye, thank you so much. I appreciate all that you have done for me."

"No problem, it was brilliant hiding the books in the car! I personally loved that they were in plain sight.

"We should be hearing from the kidnappers soon. Clarence will be setting a trap! Don't trust him to do the right thing and release your friend if he gets the books first! I presume you looked at them.

"We did! And we were thinking the same thing. Clarence will be desperate, but we must get Lavonne back, safe and sound before he gets his hands on them." I added.

Immediately after dinner, Wanda allowed herself to be put to bed. John checked her and said, "The combination of loss of blood, wine, and the mild sedative will help her sleep. She is okay but goes to the hospital in the morning!"

We were all wondering when we would get the call from the kidnappers.

Frank arrived in time to grab a plate, admitting he hadn't eaten all day. He asked me for my phone and called Ward. The FBI tech hooked it up so Ward could listen, record the conversation, and track my phone if or when I was called.

It would have been better to not have an audience for his instructions, but it was what it was. Frank said: "Maye, when they call, you will insist on talking to Lavonne. Candy Stone will take your place and make the drop".

"No way, I am the one they know and are expecting; if someone else shows up, it could put Lavonne in danger, and she will be traumatized enough!"

"They will insist that you come alone and unarmed.".... I interrupted Frank mid-sentence, saying, "But I will have my gun hidden in the car, right?" The look on my face told him I would have it with me no matter what he said.

After a big sigh, he said, "Yes, but you will not use it unless absolutely necessary! Right?" The look on his face showed me he was resigned to that possibility.

"Right!" I answered a little too quickly for his liking.

"Maye, try to convince him that you would rather drive in daylight. Lie if you have to, and do it convincingly! Spin it any way you are comfortable! Tell them you developed cataracts, and the starburst is so bad you can only drive in the daytime. We will have drones and helicopters; we want eyes on them, in daylight if possible! Ward has assigned as many officers as he can spare, and I have done the same and have borrowed some from the Phoenix Police Department. Ward is coordinating the whole thing. I will be listening in and can help you via this tiny earphone." He had me try it on, and we tested it. I had to admit it was pretty cool; I could hear him loud and clear.

"It's great! Can you hear me, too?"

"No, unfortunately, it only goes one way. Try not to let them get close enough to take your phone away from you. If it looks like they will take it or insist on tossing it out the window, switch with the extra one in your pocket.

I wanted to ask him about the chances of getting her back unharmed when the kidnappers didn't keep her blindfolded. But John had just returned from checking on Wanda and was sitting there in rapt attention, glued to our every word: I kept silent. I knew everyone else was thinking the same thing. It was good that John was oblivious to everything except the thought of having Lavonne back in his arms.

We planned to stay at Viv's for a couple hours, and if they didn't call, we would drive to Mi and Josh's house. I knew I wouldn't sleep a wink. We said our goodnights and left to hopefully shower and rest for a few minutes.

We had no sooner got in the door at Mi's when they started asking questions. Josh had set out munchies and brewed coffee, knowing we would not go to bed. Just as daylight dawned, we both had conked out, and my phone rang.

"I answered, "Hello, this is Maye West. How may I help you?"

"Well, Girly, you can help me by bringing those books if you want to see your little girlfriend alive again!"

I held the phone as he talked so Frank could hear our conversation.

"I'm not bringing them anywhere until I hear Lavonne's voice and make sure she is okay!"

"No dice, this is goin' to be played our way."

"Not going to happen! I talk to her, and she assures me she is okay, or you don't get the books, ever!" I said, raising my voice, trying to sound as strong as I thought I should.

"Look, Bitch, do you want to get her back in one piece or not?"

"I will talk to her so I know she is alive and well, or I will take the books to the police at 9AM!" And I hung up the phone.

Frank and I held our breath for several minutes until they called back.

I let it ring three times, then answered, "Hello, this is still Maye. Do we have a deal?"

"Okay, Bitch, here she is. Talk fast! We haven't got all night! *(That bastard will pay if he hurts Lavonne!)*

"Hi, Lavonne. Are you okay?"

A shaky Lavonne said, "Hello, Maye. It's good to hear your voice, even though you sound far away. Don't worry about me, I am okay. Tell

John I love him and can't wait to marry him! I don't care where or how:
I miss him so much! All four of us can fly to Vegas and get married in
one of those cute little chapels."

"Are you sure they haven't hurt you?"

"Maye, I promise they have been good to m-" The phone was
abruptly snatched out of her hand mid-word.

"Okay, this is how it will go down! If you know what is good for
you, don't try any funny stuff, or this little girl will pay for it! In exactly
one hour, you will be at Encanto Park. Park in the lot on the north
side and walk south to the first picnic area with a cover. Sit at the table
facing South! After we make sure no one follows you, I will call you!
You will stand up and hold the books high above your head so we can
see them..."

I interrupted him, saying, "Wait a minute! You mean, right now?
It's in the middle of the night! OMG! I need to get dressed!" Looking
out the window, I could see the sun, not quite peeking over the tall
trees.

"Well, Bitch, you'd better get yourself dressed and get on the road;
we ain't gonna wait all day!"

"Okay, okay! I am staying with a friend in Punkin Center; it will
take me more than an hour to get to town."

"Bitch, you better be at that park sitting at that table by 10:00 a.m.,
or the deal is off!"

"Don't be silly. I have what you want, and you have what I want!
We will exchange them at the same time, or there is no deal! I will be
there as close to 10:00 as the traffic will allow!"

"Don't forget those books!" Which was followed by a nasty laugh!"

"And you, don't forget a healthy Lavonne! Or your life won't be
worth living."

"One more thing! If you know what is good for your little friend,
don't bring the cops, and come unarmed! Got it?"

"I got it, but you get this! I will give you the books at the same time I get Lavonne!"

"Got it!" He shut the phone off!

"Maye, that was gutsy taunting him, but it may work in our favor."

"How so? Encanto park is open with not much ground cover. It will be hard to have cops close enough to be of help if they decide to shoot both of us and take the books."

"Maye, I promise we will be there, and you won't need to fire a shot!" *"Why did he look so worried? And why didn't I believe him?"*

"Frank, I plan to shove Lavonne to the ground the second I have her. I will throw the books; his attention will be on them, not us. I don't trust him as far as I can throw him! He plans on killing both of us, taking the books, and making a run for it! You guys had better be ready. If not, be prepared for a ton of paperwork because I mean to take at least one of them out if Lavonne has one scratch!"

Frank and Ward talked for several minutes. I took that time to finish dressing in loose-fitting slacks, a long-sleeved shirt with a lightweight jacket, and running shoes. Early morning can be rather chilly and windy in an open park.

I brought a heavy coat for Lavonne. She gets cold easily, and it would cushion her when I pushed her to the ground. My plan was to slip my gun into her coat pocket when I put it around her shoulders, giving me access to it when my body was her shield. My van comforted me like an old friend. I knew I would be watched; I just hoped the good guys were better shots.

I approached Encanto Park and was surprised and relieved that the parking lot was empty. I glanced around the expansive one-square-mile city block. It wasn't unusual on a weekday not to see anyone. The weekend would have been teaming with the picnic and birthday crowd.

I was 15 minutes early, and my earbuds told me they were set and gave me the go-ahead to the covered picnic area, "We will be able to hear your conversation and have eyes and ears on you!"

I walked to the table and sat on the bench seat at the end. I laid the books on the bench beside me and placed the extra coat over them. I expected to hear another car drive in the parking lot behind me. I kept glancing nervously around, trying to look calm. I was beginning to think I had been stood up when I heard a raspy voice a short distance behind me, saying, "You were supposed to hold the books up high over your head."

"Well, you were supposed to have my friend with you! Where the hell is she?"

"Right behind you!"

I started to turn around to be sure Lavonne was with him., but he shouted, "Don't turn around! Put the books on the table and shove them as far to your right as you can! Once I see they are the real ones, you will get the girl."

"Oh, no! I see Lavonne first, and you see the books after I make sure she is unharmed, or there is no deal!"

"Are you nuts, Lady? We have four people here watching you. One wrong move, and you both are toast!" *So that is what Lavonne was trying to tell us on the phone!*

"That may be true, but if you want these books, I want to see the girl before you get them. This is a quid-pro-quo deal, or it's no deal at all!" I held my breath, waiting for his next move. I heard an exasperated sigh and the crunch of shoes on gravel as he approached. I couldn't tell by the sound if Lavonne was with him. I didn't turn around or make any sudden moves. Getting shot in the back was not in my plan.

When the crunching stopped, I could feel he was close. I shifted my body to the end of the bench and slowly stood, turning to face him.

The giant facing me looked 10 feet tall and as wide as a barn, with a nasty scarred face. The shock must have shown on my face because he said, "Well, you've had a good look! Now, hand me those books!"

"That's not happening until you produce, my friend!" I knew I was playing with fire, but I had to be sure Lavonne was alive. I heard a sharp intake of breath from Frank in my ear.

"I don't see the books on the table."

"I don't see my friend?" He looked like he was going to explode. Frank said, "Maye, be careful, don't antagonize him." But I had to know Lavonne was okay! I stood my ground, staring him down.

He blinked first and stepped aside, and Lavonne was standing beside him, looking like a midget next to him.

"Okay, you can see her; where the hell are the books?"

"The books are under the coat I brought for Lavonne to put on; she gets chilled easily."

Right on cue, she began to shiver, giving me a conspiratorial look. *"Where the hell did she get all this courage?"*

"Okay, don't make any fast movements; remove them from the coat and hand them to me."

"No problem! You send Lavonne to me so I can put the coat on her. She is freezing!" I heard in my ear, "Maye, be careful!"

"You really are a mean bitch, aren't you?"

"Yes, I am! And I worked hard to earn that title!"

He heaved another big sigh and spit out, "Alright, don't make any sudden moves. The little lady will walk slowly towards you, and at the same time, you will slide those books out from under the coat and hold them up so I can look at the cover. When she gets to you, give her the jacket and then hand the books to me."

"Please let me help her put the coat on. She is so cold, she looks about ready to drop! Looking at him, pleading to allow me to put the jacket on her, was killing me. Lavonne played her part, almost like we had rehearsed.

"Alright, hurry up, I have wasted enough time. I need to get outta here before your cop buddies come roaring in with guns blazing. We don't want any stray bullets to hit either one of you, now do we?"

"I am not aware of any cops. I came here in good faith to exchange your books for my friend. I just don't want her to freeze!" Lavonne was close enough; I slipped the coat over her shoulders and my Glock in the pocket. She did well not to give me away when it pulled the shoulder down a bit.

"Okay, you got your little girl! Now toss those books over to me, and I will be on my way." In my ear, I heard, "Maye, when you toss the books high enough to make him scramble to catch them, and while he struggles, get Lavonne to the other side of the table and drop to the ground, fast!"

Lavonne's shivering stopped the minute the coat was on her shoulders, and she wrapped it around herself. I picked up the books to toss them like Frank wanted, but I didn't imagine a man his size could move that fast! The big bastard was standing right in front of me, reaching for the books! He bent to pick them up, pausing to read the cover.

I heard a deafening shout, "MOVE!" In my ear, I am surprised he couldn't hear it, too!

I grabbed Lavonne in my arms and bolted around the bench, falling to the ground under the seat, covering Lavonne with my body. I heard the boards of the table and the bench I was cowering under exploding! It didn't afford much protection; I silently thanked Frank for ordering me to wear the vest! Holding my body up so I didn't crush Lavonne, I felt several bullets hitting me in the back; the pain was paralyzing! Before I could recover from the shock, several more found their mark, and I lapsed into unconsciousness, not knowing how many hit the vest and how many hit me!

The last thing I remember thinking is, *"Please, let Lavonne be okay!"*

The drones observed the guys sneaking into the park. And clearly saw their pathetic attempts to hide behind the few bushes and trees. Lavonne was wrong about four men being ready for the handoff, but it didn't matter. Our team had them covered and prepared to intercept them when needed. Seeing the big man step up close to Maye, I screamed into the mike, "Watch out, Number 1 is on the move!" He snuck up next to Maye while she was putting that silly coat on Lavonne! "Everyone! Protect those two at all costs."

"Relax, Frank, we have eyes on them!

"Thanks, buddy!"

"When I saw that big guy standing next to Maye, my only thought was, OMG, I can't lose Maye! And then I saw that big guy grab the books before Maye could throw them up in the air like she was planning. I held my breath when I saw Maye grab Lavonne and sprint for the other side of the bench! I was horrified when I saw Maye push Lavonne to the ground and cover her with her own body! She was protecting Lavonne from the barrage of bullets aimed at them!

"Maye, are you alright? Dammit! Maye, speak to me!"

"Frank! Wait, stay down! Maye shot that big guy right between the eyes! There aren't any others close to them. We have 8 in custody, but we need to get them all and secure those books!

"*The hell with the damn books!*" I couldn't stand it another minute; I jumped up and took off on a dead run toward Maye! I could see her still covering Lavonne with her body, but neither one was moving! I ran at a break-neck speed, hardly breathing until I saw Lavonne struggling from under Maye. I knew the impact of several bullets hitting Maye's vest would stun her for a few minutes, but she should be coming around by now unless a shot got around the vest!

I felt a stinging pain in the fleshy part of my thigh, and my body involuntarily stumbled to the ground, ass over teakettle! Ward told me later it saved my life as the next bullet would have hit me in the upper body or my head. I didn't care; I had to get to Maye! I hesitated long enough to hear Ward call the all-clear; I was off at a limping run, blood shooting out of my leg wound.

Reaching her, I screamed into the mike, "Ward, we need an ambulance. There is too much blood! The big guy is lying across the table, bleeding! I think Maye and Lavonne both have been hit! For God's sake, Hurry!"

"Hang in there, Frank! Three are on the way! A couple of my guys were hit, too! Can you tell how bad either of them is hit?"

"Don't know yet!" I rolled Maye off Lavonne and was shocked to see Maye's Glock in a shaking Lavonne's hand! I gently took the warm gun from her hand, put the safety on, and put it in my pocket.

"Lavonne, are you okay?"

"Of course I am! Maye saved me! That big guy was planning on killing both of us! When Maye was shoving me to the ground, I got her gun out of my pocket and shot him. I don't know if I hit him; I am not very good with guns. Maye isn't answering me! OMG, there is blood everywhere! I don't think I am hurt or feel any pain. Noooo, it must be Maye!"

"You did real good, honey, don't worry. Ambulances are on the way. Just sit on the bench while I check Maye."

Maye appeared to be unaware of me rolling her over and checking her body for wounds. I could see blood coming from somewhere, but I couldn't tell where with the vest on. I didn't want to take it off because the snugness might slow the bleeding. I heard the screams of the ambulances and stood up, frantically signaling them to hurry.

The EMT attendant asked me what kind of gun she was shot with; I said most of the guys had handguns. Checking her pressure and vitals, they started an IV, immediately loaded her into the ambulance, and sped to the hospital.

I tried to get into the ambulance with them, but they needed the room. One EMT gave me his necktie, and Lavonne wound it around my leg. I commandeered the closest vehicle, but Lavonne argued me out of driving.

"You will be dangerous to us and other vehicles; now move over! I want to get to the hospital in one piece!"

As she sped up the highway, she demanded, "Call John, and put the phone on speaker!"

The minute he answered, I said, "John, Lavonne is safe and was not hurt; she is driving me to the hospital. I only have a scratch on my leg, but Maye was shot!"

I leaned back and closed my eyes, holding the phone so Lavonne could talk to John.

"John, Maye covered me with her body! She saved my life! I don't know her condition, but I am staying at the hospital until I find out. I love you and can't wait to feel your arms around me. Don't worry, honey, I am okay!"

John shouted, "I am on the way; everyone is coming. We are bringing Wanda to be checked out; she was shot getting the books out of the hiding place."

"Oh! John, Frank, made Maye wear a vest that gave her some protection." Before she thought about me being with her, she said, "There was a lot of blood, but I think I shot the bastard that shot Maye! She put her gun in my pocket, and I fired one shot before she landed on top of me."

I roused enough to say, "Hey, John, you and Maye will be proud of Lavonne; that guy had at least one shot right between the eyes!"

Lavonne and John laughed and talked all the way to the hospital. All I could think of was all that blood, and someone had better be able to tell me what was going on with Maye when I got there!

The drive to the hospital seemed like hours! I helped Lavonne out of the car, and I limped/raced with her to find Maye was already in surgery, and no one could or would tell me anything. Lavonne paced the waiting room while I leaned against a wall, trying not to pass out; the necktie did its job and slowed blood flow to a minimum.

The first to arrive was the crew from James and Viv's house. John only had eyes and arms for Lavonne; they embraced each other and cried. John only paused long enough to direct Jeb to escort Wanda to a nurse and to be sure she got to the ER. She was admitted for surgery. John was right; she had fragments in her leg. Fred arrived and took over Jeb's duty, waiting for Wanda to come out of the operation.

Ward and Candy Stone arrived a few minutes later, and he attempted to give me the info on the clean-up of the men in the park. I wish I could say I was interested, but my mind could only process Maye was shot! Ward realized I was not able to handle anything but Maye's condition. He gave up trying to tell me what happened.

I limped across the floor until Ward stepped in front of me, putting his hands on my shoulders, saying, "Buddy, come with me; we need to allow someone to attend to that wound on your leg!"

"It's nothing, only a scratch!"

"Really? Then, who do you think is bleeding all over the floor?"

"Uh!" Looking down, I said, "Sorry, I didn't mean to make a mess."

Ward left me in the ER, and he and Candy joined the others in the waiting room. John and Lavonne entertained everyone with the details of her capture and the big shoot-out! Ward and Candy filled in the rest of the action.

Lavonne only cried when she looked at John with those big blue eyes and said, "They took my beautiful ring!"

"It's okay, sweetheart! We will get you another one?"

"That won't be necessary; we confiscated it and will release it to you as soon as the paperwork is done," Ward said.

John shook his hand, saying, "Thanks, we had it made for her; it is one of a kind like she is!" Looking at her with so much love, Lavonne's tears finally fell. And her body collapsed in his arms. He carried her to a couch, and everyone gathered around, helping with pillows and a warm blanket. John knelt by her on the floor, adding his tears to hers, murmuring soft words until she calmed down, let exhaustion take over, and fell asleep.

Chapter 17 Maye, Wanda, and Frank are out of surgery.

Oblivious to everyone, John held Lavonne, not stirring when Mi and Josh arrived. The group walked the floor or sat, waiting for news of Maye, Wanda, and Frank! The hours ticked by until Jeb and George appeared with boxes laden with drinks, sandwiches, and snacks, slightly lightening the mood.

"No word on our patients?" they asked.

"Not a peep. I think I will wander to the nursing station to see if I can find out anything." Mi said. She and Josh returned several minutes later with Frank in a wheelchair, his right leg elevated to nearly waist height! To his startled audience, he said, "See, I told you, it was just a scratch!"

Josh tattled on him, telling them, "Yeah, just a scratch! He flatly refused to let them operate to remove the shrapnel until after Maye is out of surgery."

"I'm not sure how you talked the Doctor into delaying surgery, but I guarantee you will be on your way back the minute Maye wakes up! You do remember she carries a gun, don't you?" Ward laughed.

"I do, but she will be in bed, and I sent her gun to ballistics for testing. I might need a little help from my friends."

That exchange lightened the mood for a few minutes. The hours of doing nothing but waiting started making everyone sleepy. By the time the sun peeked over the horizon, most visitors were in various states of sleep.

Frank was leaning back in the wheelchair and had just closed his eyes. Hearing footsteps, he jerked awake and wheeled over to the Doctor, looking up with expectation in his eyes.

"I have news about Ms. West. Are her relatives here or on the way?"

"No, Ms. West doesn't have any family! We all are her family; you can tell us about her condition." Frank said, swinging his arm out in a wide arc to show how many people were waiting for news.

"Are you her husband?"

Hearing the conversation between Frank and the Doctor, Lavonne jumped up and hurried over to them.

"How is Maye? Can we see her now?" She said in her most pathetic voice, looking up with those big blue eyes that usually melt hearts.

"I am sorry, Miss, the hospital only allows relatives of a patient in the ICU." He looked apologetic but firm."

Frank wheeled close, and he looked up at him and said, "Look, I know this is unusual, but Ms. West and I are planning to be married, so give a guy a break. At least tell me her condition!"

Ward showed his ID, saying, "Doctor, that woman was instrumental in capturing a lot of bad guys last night, and she used her body to shield this woman!" Putting his hand on Lavonne's shoulder! These two people are as close to Maye as any relative can be, so please at least tell them her condition, the FBI, and I will be grateful."

Dr. Sorenson hesitated and said, "I suppose you will repeat everything I say to all those standing here looking like deer in headlights." He raised his voice so all could hear and said, "Hello folks, Ms. West was shot multiple times." Knowing a million questions were right behind the communal intake of breath, he held up his hand. "It was fortunate that she was wearing the vest, and the bullets were from handguns." You could almost feel some of the tension leaving the audience.

"Ms. West was shot in her right arm, but no bone damage was present. The vest protected her main body. The bullets were fired at angles that allowed two shots to travel under it. They pierced her abdomen but were slowed down by the vest, but still did considerable damage. We repaired the damage, and she will be fine. I am sorry to say she cannot have babies."

Frank and Lavonne stared like statues until he said, "Ms. West will be fine, and under the circumstances, I am going to allow the two of you to see her, and only for a couple of minutes!"

Before anyone could move, Lavonne moved in front of Frank, standing with her hands on her hips, and said, "Mister, I heard what you said about getting married! I hope that Maye's not being able to give you babies makes any difference. You'd better not break her heart, or you will have me to contend with!"

Frank was flustered, with all eyes on him, and he strained to get close to her and said, "Lavonne, you know, I have loved Maye forever; I just got her to think about marriage a few weeks ago. You all know about our secret arrangement; she was just starting to like it. I love her and don't care if there are babies! If she wants them, we can adopt them! Can I go see my soon-to-be wife now? Please?"

Lavonne threw her arms around his neck and kissed him on the cheek, giggling at his red face. "Come on, Bro, let's check on my Sista!"

Before Frank wheeled into Maye's room, he managed to get his leg down so Maye wouldn't know he had delayed surgery to come to visit her. Lavonne knew his deception would be useless. Maye would figure it out the minute she saw him.

They reached the ICU and were stopped by a nurse looking at them like they were playing hooky from school!

She asked, "Has Dr. Sorensen permitted you to visit Mrs. West?"

Before Frank or Lavonne could open their mouths, the Dr. arrived and told her to allow the two of them for a few minutes. She looked at her watch so they knew she would be timing them.

Frank wheeled close on one side, holding Maye's hand, Lavonne on the other. She wasn't intubated but had oxygen. They were shocked when they saw the number of IV bags attached to the tall pole.

They were both excited when she moved her fingers in their hands, and they smiled.

Lavonne said, "Maye, I will check on the progress of your new offices, and if they are done, I will start putting all the fancy stuff in your apartment!" She giggled when she heard a tiny mumble.

"You rest, Hon; I promise to watch her and won't let her put any ruffles and bows in our apartment. We can't stay very long tonight, but we will be back."

They returned to the waiting room and told everyone that she was not awake but would be tomorrow and hopefully could have visitors.

Mi offered to bring some of her things from home. Frank thanked her and was reluctantly pushed back to the ER for his much-needed operation. He agreed, only because he would be near Maye. Frank worried Lavonne would be planning a double wedding. He and Maye will have to nip that in the bud after blabbing to the world that he loved Maye and wanted to marry her.

Lavonne, John, Mi, Josh, Jeb, and George decided to check on Wanda. Fred was still waiting for the Doctor to allow him to see her. Ward had stationed two detectives outside her door, and they wouldn't let Fred in until the Dr. gave permission. The Dr. gave the same instructions, only two at a time and only for a few minutes. Lavonne and Fred entered her room to find her awake and talkative. She reviewed the whole thing and was excited to hear Lavonne's story. Lavonne hugged her and thanked her for helping to free her.

When they came out, everyone departed for home to get some much-needed sleep, promising to return in the morning.

Once Ward and Candy watched Frank wheeled into surgery, they left to go home and get some sleep, as did the rest of the crew.

Ward and Candy arrived early the next morning despite the late night. Ward formed a task force to investigate everyone named in the books, no matter how insignificant they seemed. This included the people named either as co-conspirators or victims of blackmail. They intended to dig into every aspect of his operation. They were anxious to build a solid case against Clarence Poole! For a crook, he was extremely well organized. Ward planned to spend most of his time in this room, supervising the work and reviewing the information gathered.

Ward and Candy planned an evening hospital visit to check on their friends and Wanda. His and Frank's officers had been released and were home recuperating. He fully expected Frank to be out of the hospital and back at work by tomorrow.

Clarence wasn't going down without a fight! When he learned the books were still in the Phoenix Police Department's hands and his men were in jail, he told his lawyer to set plans in motion to use his "get out of jail free" card. Clarence decided that taking out Maye, Frank, and Wanda simultaneously would cause excitement and muddy the water! He wanted revenge, and it would be fun to shake up the whole bunch of cops, but saving his own skin was a top priority! If his other plans were successful, their demise would be his going-away present. He concentrated on the books because he felt the copies would mean nothing without them! When he heard that the books were taken to the sheriff's office, not the FBI building, he was a happy camper and sped up his timeline.

Maye woke up the next morning when the nurse came in to check on her vitals. Looking around, she saw white walls and heard machines beeping.

"How bad was I hurt?" she said groggily. She tried to feel her body and see for herself how bad she was hurt, but one arm was held rigidly on a board with an IV inserted. Focusing her eyes, she was horrified at the number of bags of medicine hanging on the metal rod above her head. She felt more bandages than she thought there should be. The nurse, seeing her checking her body, said, "You are in ICU, and you are going to be okay. Relax. The Doctor will come in soon, and he will tell you about your condition."

"Condition? That doesn't sound like a good thing! OMG, I must have been shot, but how can that be? Frank made me wear that blasted vest that hindered me when I dove under the bench! My God, I need to find out if

Lavonne is alright! She has to be okay!" Maye fretted until Dr. Sorenson finally came in.

The first thing out of her mouth before he could get in the door and sit down beside her bed was, "Doctor, is Lavonne okay?"

"Relax, she is fine; you covered her well; she only had the wind knocked out of her and is home getting a good night's sleep," Before he could tell her more, she interrupted him again, "What about Wanda? Was anyone else shot?"

"Ms. West, everyone is fine. Now, can I tell you about your condition?"

She swallowed her questions and kept quiet.

"You were lucky to have had that vest on because you were hit several times in the back, which knocked you out. Your back will be sore for some time. However, because of the angle, two of the bullets missed the vest, requiring some repair to your abdomen."

"What does that mean?

"It was necessary to do a complete hysterectomy."

Maye was quiet for such a long time the Doctor became worried, so he continued, "I talked to your fiance, and he assured your friend Lavonne that he didn't care if you had babies; you could adopt."

"What! Lavonne and Frank were talking about babies?"

"I could only let them in the ICU if they were family. Mr. Stone assured me that you and Frank are getting married, and Lavonne is like your Sister.

Maye, now fully awake, started laughing but quickly stopped, "Oww, that hurts!"

Holding her stomach, she said, "God, I wish I had been awake to hear that conversation! I suppose she is planning a big double cowboy wedding! We are gonna have to nip that one in the bud! I love her to pieces, but she is my cutest pain in the ass and has been for a hundred years. Speaking of Frank, where is he? I am surprised he isn't here sleeping in a chair!"

"Mr. Singleton was wounded in the leg and had surgery last night after he made sure that you were going to be okay. He is resting comfortably and can come to see you as soon as he is healed enough for crutches."

"He is healed enough for a chair, only because your nurse wouldn't let me have crutches!" Said a voice behind them as Frank rolled through the door with a big smile.

Dr. Sorenson said, "I will let you two visit for a while, but you both need to rest, so the nurse will break this up and send you back to your room, Mr. Singleton.

As soon as the Doctor was out the door, I said, "I know you, Mister! If they don't tie you to the bed, you will have those crutches by this afternoon and back to work! You need to take care of yourself! I understand that we are engaged to be married, and if I know Miss Lavonne, she is planning a big double cowboy wedding!" I started laughing, holding my stomach, and grimacing with pain.

"Oh, I guess since I announced it, we will have to go through with it. I said that to get by the 'only relatives' thing, to visit you, and Lavonne was so thrilled, I didn't have the heart to rain on her parade. We agreed to the trial marriage, and it looked like you were starting to like it a little. I know I like it a lot! We will have a heart-to-heart talk with Lavonne as soon as we get out of here unless you aren't interested in making it permanent, ever!" He said, afraid of what her answer would be, but he had to know.

"I know the Dr. told you I won't have any babies. Are you sure you won't want some little Singletons to carry on your name sometime down the road?"

"You are all I need! But if you want kids, we can adopt."

"You are enough for me, too!"

"Good, I can't wait for both of us to get out of here and move into that apartment Lavonne is decorating with all that cute stuff!"

"She'd better not! I will personally tear them all down!

"Honey, don't worry. I will go by as soon as I get out of here and check it out. I don't think Lavonne will have time. She is busy telling everyone what a hero you are!

The nurse came in and scooted Frank out, and within minutes, I fell asleep and slept off and on for most of the day. Frank visited Wanda before he was taken to his room, and the wheelchair was taken away so he would rest.

Both Frank and Maye rested for the rest of the day. Early evening, Josh and Mi came with the things Maye would need for her stay in the hospital. Lavonne and John visited for a short time. At bedtime, Frank was reluctantly escorted out by the nurse and confined to his room. Frank was determined to be released, or he was sneaking out in the morning.

Chapter 18 Clarence plays his get-out-of-jail FREE Card!

Frank adamantly refused the wheel chair or crutches the following morning. He grudgingly agreed to accept a cane, which would be standing in the corner of his office. He visited Maye, not mentioning that he was supposed to spend a few days at home, hoping her gun would still be in evidence when she found out.

Mary Anne was surprised to see Frank, "Are you supposed to be out of the hospital?"

"I was released and only need the cane. I came by to see if Maye's apartment is finished, and Lavonne was faithful to her word, and it is minus the fluff!"

She decided he looked a little shaky and said, "I have wanted to see it myself. Do you mind if I will go with you?"

"Okay, but I don't need any help."

She wanted to make sure he didn't fall down the stairs. He made the stairs to the apartment without panting for breath but was grateful for Mary Anne's arm around him.

Frank was pleased with the king-size beds, the weight bench, and the treadmill. The upgraded hot tub, a sauna, and the comfortable couch in front of the 65-inch screen TV above the large gas log fireplace will be welcome!

Looking down at Mary Anne, he said more to himself than her, "I could move my stuff in and put the Condo on the market before Maye gets home and save her the trouble."

Mary Anne said, "The Real Estate Market is so hot right now, you might net 2 or 3 times what you paid for your Condo. But might want to wait and have Maye list it for you!"

"You're right! She would kick my ass out before I got settled!"

"Frank, tell me the truth about Maye; how bad was she hurt?

"I don't know much more than what the Doctor told us the other night. She is a private person; she might open up to Lavonne or you more than she will to me."

"Maye is a logical person; give her time."

"I hope so because, until the Doctor said we can't have babies, we never thought or talked about them. I am happy with our lives the way they are right now!"

"She is one brave, strong woman! Don't worry about her; she will be all right!"

Frank agreed, saying, "You aren't so bad yourself." Which brought a big smile to her face. He managed the first 4 or 5 steps by himself, but he gratefully leaned on her for balance when he felt her arm slip around his waist.

They toured the new offices and the breakroom. Frank whistled at the size, envisioning Christmas, other parties, and lunches.

"Thanks for the tour, Mary Anne; Maye will love this! I'd better get going; I will be back tonight. Did they change all the locks when they finished the remodeling?"

"No, you can use your key, but the new alarm system is a little tricky, so I will go over it with you before you leave. You will stay home for a few days, won't you?"

"Nope! I have things to do, and I will visit Maye tonight."

He drove to his condo and, with difficulty, packed most of his clothes, loaded them into the back of his car, planning on moving in tonight after he visited Maye. He would use the guest bedroom. He wanted to wait to sleep in her Mistress bedroom until he could sleep with her. He thought, "*Hell, I might carry her across the threshold!*" That brought a smile to his face.

Arriving at the office, Shirl chided him for being there. Frank said, "I recall you coming in on crutches in pajama bottoms, balking at desk duty."

"Yeah, and I recall you ordering Officer Brenda to shoot me if I got out of the car!"

"That was the best order I ever gave; I still wonder why she failed to follow it!"

"It was touch and go for a while; I waited in the car until she gave permission for me to get out when we got to James's house."

"Come on, let's head to the Task Force room to see what is happening with the books. You can fill me in on any new developments on the way."

Frank settled into his favorite chair, reading reports until his eyes matched his tired body. He leaned back in his chair, closing his eyes for a few minutes.

He was dreaming about a cup of coffee when a steaming cup appeared in front of him. Looking up, he saw Officer Brenda with a smile a mile wide. He drank deeply, feeling the energy surge back into his tired body.

"This is your reward for making me the winner of the office pool!"

"Office pool?"

"I bet you would be in the office the minute you got out of the hospital, and I won 50 bucks! I also saw your cane in your office in the corner," she said, hooking it on the arm of his chair.

"Thanks, guess I forgot it."

"Yeah, I know! I heard Lavonne is as good a shot as Maye! You guys had all the excitement; it has been pretty dull here. Clarence was a busy guy; he had his hands into many fires."

"Don't tell me that you admire him?"

"No, and I don't think he is done! I think he will make another attempt to get those books and seek revenge, probably at the same time!"

"We are pretty secure here. But, if you are right, maybe we should take some precautions. Any suggestions?"

"I would have the original books placed in a more secure lock-up; we only need the copies for our investigation.

"You make a good argument. I will have a chat with Ward Stone; he may have some ideas."

He no sooner finished that statement when Ward came through the door, exclaiming, "What the heck are you doing here? Aren't you supposed to be home, resting?"

"It was just a flesh wound; the doctor was over-cautious. We've got work to do. Is one of those Starbucks coffees for me?"

"Absolutely!"

"Thanks! Officer Brenda suggests we put Clarence's original books in a secure vault. She thinks Clarence will make another attempt to get them and seek revenge. What do you think?"

"I agree, he will try something; he is still behind bars, and eight of his men are cooling their heels in jail, awaiting trial."

While they were talking and enjoying their coffee, Officer Brenda picked up the phone, and they heard her saying, "Certainly, he is here; I will put you through."

"Sir, John Grissom, the warden at Florence prison, is on the phone."

"Hello, John," Frank said and then listened for several minutes until he said, "Son of a Bitch! When did that happen?" He listened for several more minutes and said, "Send me all the information and videos, and thanks for the heads up."

"We've got trouble! Clarence has disappeared from prison."

"Define disappeared? He couldn't just walk out! What happened?"

"It was a busy day, and there were a lot of visitors. Three men came in separately and didn't attract the guards' notice. One of the men had facial hair and wore a cap with hair to his collar. There was a noisy skirmish among several other visitors, and it took the guards several minutes to quiet it down. During that time, one of the men stripped off his clothes and underneath was wearing a replica of Clarence's prison garb. When he took off his cap, the hair came with it, and he bore a close enough resemblance to Clarence; no one noticed. The facial hair was glued on Clarence, and with the man's clothes over his uniform, he walked out.

Ward and Brenda both said, "Son of a bitch."

"The videos must have caught him changing clothes?" Brenda exclaimed.

"While the skirmish was going on, two large men stood in front of the camera. At first, it looked like they huddled in the corner to be out of the fighting on the video. Still, it was obvious that they were shielding the men, changing clothes and facial disguises on close inspection." Frank said while running his fingers through his hair!

"He is forwarding the information, including videos; they should be here now. Officer Brenda, can you set up the videos?" Frank said.

"Yes, Sir!"

The three watched the video twice. After the second time and more expletives, they grudgingly concluded that the scenario was damned smart.

"We need to get those books somewhere secure, like Fort Knox! Frank said.

"The FBI building is close! Clarence would have to employ a crew of mercenaries to break in, and that would be a formidable challenge." Ward offered.

"The only challenge will be getting them from here to your building." Frank mused, sipping his coffee.

"I can have three armored vehicles with armed guards deliver them to our building," Ward said as he dialed his phone. He paused, saying, Is the first thing in the morning okay, or do you think sooner?"

"Ordinarily, I would agree to morning, but in light of the prison break, I think

now would be better than later!" Frank said, and Brenda nodded in agreement.

Ward amended instructions, and when he hung up, he smiled, saying, "They are on the way!"

Frank jumped up, saying, "OMG, Maye and Wanda are in danger!"

"Settle down, Frank; I assigned agents to the hospital. The Doctor was helpful, giving my guys a list with pictures of the personnel that should have a reason to go into their rooms. He also had Wanda moved next to Maye to make guarding them easier. They both asked for their guns, and you can relax; they didn't get them."

"You are one brave man. I don't see any bruises or bandages. How did you get them to agree?"

"I promised them, if there was any trouble, my guys would give them guns to defend themselves."

Brenda and Frank laughed, "They didn't buy that, did they?"

"I'm not sure, but they didn't have guns when I left."

"Did you warn your officers?"

The look on Ward's face made them both snort!

Brenda said, "I will put together the stack of paperwork for civilians firing guns and shooting criminals. By the end of the night, you might need them!" Brenda was still laughing when she went out of the door.

Frank slumped down, running his fingers through his hair.

"Buddy, relax! The vans will pull into the back of the building, and once the books are on board, it will take an army to get them," Ward said, putting his hand on Frank's shoulder to calm him.

The FBI's solid concrete building was only three blocks from the old brick building housing the Sheriff's Department. Frank called in as many off-duty officers as he could and put the building on red alert! Officers Shirl and Brenda instructed the additional officers to be prepared for an assault. Snipers were stationed on the roof, and it seemed like hours before Officers Brenda and Shirl came through the door, saying, "Three armored vans entered the underground garage.

The driver of the middle vehicle said to let you and Ward know they were there. We shut and locked the doors."

"We need to get those books into the trucks and back on the road. Officer Brenda interrupted him, "Sir, one of our snipers reported movement on the roof of the building east of us."

"Damn, we're too late! Barricade the doors; the trucks just came through! Station officers at all windows and tell them to stay out of sight. Do not shoot until I give the order and report any street movement to us!"

Ward ordered his men out of the vehicles and stationed them as backup to Frank's men. Two men entered the task room with their arms full of weapons, handing them out.

Frank suddenly jumped out of his chair and asked Officer Brenda, "Where in the hell are those books?"

"They are still locked in the Evidence Room."

"They need to be transferred to one of those vans, now!"

Overhearing the conversation, Ward sent a couple of his men to accompany Officer Brenda and guard the van with the books!"

"I have no problem with the extra guns, but do you think they will try to breach our building?" Ward asked.

"Yes, I do! Clarence doesn't know you are here with backup! It could get noisy and messy for a while.

"I have alerted my boss to be ready to come to our aid," Ward added.

Officer Brenda called to tell Frank the books were safe in the van.

Chapter 19 Assault on the Sherriff's Building

Maye's mind was in two places and uneasy in both. Slipping out of bed, Wanda quietly entered Maye's room, hoping not to wake her. She couldn't help laughing, seeing her standing beside her bed in her bathrobe.

"Maye, how did you talk the nurse into taking the IV out, or did you do it?"

"I am a patient; a nurse must have done it! Wanda, I might ask you the same question."

"Of course, a nurse must have removed it."

"Uh, huh! Have you heard anything about what is happening?"

"Not a peep, but something is up! Frank would be here sitting beside my bed! Ward gave up way too easily, promising us guns. They think the action is happening at the precinct; I think they are wrong!"

"I agree; Clarence will send men to capture or kill us. We have to get guns now!"

"Wanda, do you have a plan to get them?"

"At this moment, I don't have one, but why don't I invite those nice agents in for a chat?"

Wanda peeked out the door, beckoning to the guys. They glanced at each other before following her inside. They stood at attention with their backs to the door.

Maye approached the first man, asking, "Frank hasn't called me this morning. Do you know what is keeping him so busy? Should I be worried?"

He swallowed and said, "Ma'am, you have nothing to worry about; everything is going according to plan."

"What plan is that exactly?" she asked, cocking her head, looking him right in the eye.

Wanda walked close to the second young man, getting in his face and saying, "Now look here, I am supposed to testify in one of the most prominent trials for this area! How many agents besides you two guys are here to protect us?"

The younger of the two officers remembered hearing about Maye West, the woman standing in front of him with fists pressed to her hips! He was so tall Maye had to stand on tippy-toes to look into his baby face, which sported a deep frown. She said, "In case you haven't noticed, neither of us can run very fast, and Clarence's men will be well-armed mercenaries! We need weapons NOW!"

Ward's orders echoed in their heads! "The women can ONLY be given weapons IF there was a clear and present danger to them!" They also remembered him saying, if those women are injured in any way, your ass is grass!

The men hesitated for a couple of seconds. They took revolvers and a box of shells out of their backpacks for each woman. The women checked to be sure they were loaded and stuffed them in their robe pockets, making their bathrobes droop on one side.

Maye and Wanda, facing the men, said, "Now tell us the truth about what is happening at the precinct!"

"Okay, you don't need to worry about Clarence's prison break last night! The precinct is prepared for a siege by Clarence and his men. He will be unsuccessful; three armored cars were sent to transfer the books to the FBI building but stayed for backup. You girls can relax. We will be right outside the door."

The guys, now assured by the women they were not worried and thanked for the guns, went back to their stations.

Frank relaxed as much as he could while mentally checking and re-checking the preparations. He suspected Ward was doing the same thing. The silence was deafening! He felt they could have held off an assault by Clarence's men, but the extra FBI officers gave him confidence they had the upper hand. He was dead-tired and was holding it together between strong coffee and sheer determination. He was grateful that Maye was safely in the hospital, with guards and no gun!

Satisfied he had done everything possible, Frank leaned back in his chair and closed his eyes for a moment. He smiled, picturing the surprise Clarence's men would receive against the three complements of FBI agents and the extra men he called up. He was startled awake by the smell of hot burgers, fries, and fresh hot coffee on his desk. Officer Shirl said, "Boss, you probably haven't eaten all day."

"Thanks, we both needed this," Ward said, sitting across from him, enjoying his meal. "It looks like Clarence's men are waiting for the cover of darkness to make their move! I wish they would get on with it; waiting is tiresome."

The door opened, and Officer Brenda came in and sat down, "I decided to join your guys for lunch. The guys in the van are all having burritos. I think it will be safer here with you, as she unwrapped her burger and took a big bite.

"I have been thinking about Clarence's push to get his books! We know he wants them bad enough to attempt an ambush on the sheriff's building. I've been thinking. He vowed revenge on anyone who helped Wanda, right? Well, who are the major players? He knows that we already have had a good look at the books. He probably has figured that we made copies! What does he want more? His hands on those books or revenge?" How many guards are at the hospital guarding Maye and Wanda?

Ward and Frank dropped their burgers on the table, looking at each other wide-eyed, "OMG!" They both mumbled through mouths full of burgers, "We sent two green kids to guard them because we were so sure he would try for the books first! We didn't think about him hitting both at once!" We need to send people to protect them NOW!"

Officer Brenda calmly wiped her face with her napkin and said, "If Clarence sees a bunch of cars leaving this building, he will know something is up. How about we take two civilian cars with four people in each car in civilian clothes? We aren't far from the hospital and will look like visitors. If I am right, Maye and Wanda are already armed and will need backup!"

"Officer Brannen, you and Officer Packard pick 4 officers, get to the hospital, and make sure Maye and Wanda are safe. We will hold down the fort, but I need to know the minute you are in position and keep us informed."

Grabbing their burgers and drinks, the officers walked briskly out the door. Within minutes, they had picked their crew and were headed for the hospital. When they arrived, they split up into groups of two officers each. They left four officers to scout each hospital floor to check for anyone who didn't look like they belonged. They took the elevator to Wanda and Maye's floor and approached the two officers guarding the women's rooms.

Shirl and Brenda showed their badges to the two guards and introduced themselves. The first guard said, "I am Roy, and this is Ben. Boy, are we glad to see you guys! We are starved; can we run and grab a burger?"

Roy looked like a peach-fuzzed-faced teenager, towering over Shirl with a shock of blond hair and pale blue eyes. Ben was nearly the opposite, with buzz-cut dark brown hair and soft brown eyes.

"How are Wanda and Maye doing? Have they conned you out of guns yet?" Brenda asked.

Roy bowed and said, "Yeah, we decided, rather than argue with them, it would be better to give in. Our Boss said to give them guns only if there was danger. They convinced us that Clarence might attack the sheriff's building and make a run at the women at the same time. I hope we don't get into too much trouble." He said as he swallowed.

"You did well. We came to the same conclusion and brought 4 officers stationed nearby, ready to help. Go ahead and grab a sandwich and get back ASAP. We may need you soon." The guys took off, and two other guys took their places. Shirl knocked gently on the door to Maye's room, saying, "Maye, it's Officer Packard and Brannen. May we come in?" They breathed heavily, ready to face the music.

"Yes," was the answer.

Maye was sitting on her bed with the head cranked up as high as possible, in a bathrobe, smiling. "Hi guys, we were wondering when you would show up."

"Yeah, what took you so long?" came a voice from nowhere.

Wanda slid off the mattress under the bed and stood beside Maye, both grinning like Cheshire cats.

"It was Brenda's idea; it was taking Clarence's men too long to attack, and she figured he might want revenge almost as much as he wanted the books."

"Good call; we were getting a little worried that they might make a run on both of us at the same time, so we decided to improvise."

"Wait a minute! Maye, isn't it a little early for you to have your IVs out?" Officer Brenda said.

"She is a stubborn woman! I tried to tell her that it was a bad idea!" Wanda said.

"Shut up; I notice you don't have one, either! What is your plan? Are his men here yet? Maye said, hopping off the bed, wincing when her feet hit the floor, and she stood up.

"The plan is, you two stay here! Officers are scouting the building. We think he will hit us with half a dozen mercenaries in both rooms at once. They will assume you both will be in bed and easy pickin's with six armed men against two unarmed women.

"They'll try to nab us first and take us to Clarence for fun and games if he is not with them. If Clarence is with them, the party will be right here! If we put up a fight, they will kill us, quick and get out." Wanda said.

Brenda and Shirl took Wanda's mattress back to her room, helped her to make the bed, and put her in a sitting position. Brenda stayed with Wanda, and Shirl stayed with Maye.

Nerves were on high alert, and when a knock sounded, they snapped to attention.

A nurse saw the full IV bag and realized it should be nearly empty. She picked up Maye's wrist and asked, "Who authorized taking out your IV?"

"I did. It would interfere with my gun hand," Maye said.

"Why would you need a gun? You should be resting."

"I will, as soon as my visitors arrive."

"Visiting hours isn't until 7:00; now you should relax," as she started to lower the head of the bed.

May put her hand on the nurse's arm, stopping her. "Leave my bed alone and leave my room; the visitors I am expecting will be armed and dangerous,"

She said as she pulled her gun out from under the bedding, and the nurse's face paled.

Shirl was instantly at her side, taking the nurse by the arm, leading her to the door, and gently pushing her out. He told the guys to not let anyone in either room.

Maye relaxed, putting her gun away, and Shirl walked back by the door.

When they heard gunshots from the other room, Shirl bolted for the hall door, and Maye limped to the dividing door! Shirl and the extra guard ran through the open door, seeing a pleased Wanda still in bed, with blood trickling down one arm. Looking around, they saw two guys slumped against the wall, with blood splattered across the floor. One of the agents had sunk to the floor with blood seeping from his shoulder.

Wanda was sitting on her bed, still pointing her gun at the intruders, covering the officer who was checking them for weapons. Shirl said, "Good shots, Wanda! They are both dead."

"Damn, I let them get a couple shots off, a good thing it's only a scratch! How is the agent?

The young officer looked up at her, smiling, and said, "It's just a flesh wound; thanks for the help!"

Holding onto the door frame, Maye saw a Nurse push past Brenda to bind Wanda's arm.

Two guards pushed two more men in cuffs through the door and said, "We have two more men downstairs. We are sure we have all of them, but we will check the grounds and leave a couple officers outside and on your doors.

Officer Brenda put her arm around Maye and led her back to bed. She pressed the call button, and a nurse came in and replaced the IV. Maye didn't have much fight left, and before Brenda left the room, she was asleep, and Wanda was on her way to the ER and probably more surgery.

Officer Brenda gave the two young recruits the honor of continuing to guard the women. She and Shirl put the remaining men in an unmarked car to be transported to the Sheriff's office.

When they arrived, they went to the task force office and reported to Frank. "Two of the men are dead, and the other four are in cells downstairs."

Before they could explain, Frank burst out, "Who shot them?"

"Sir, Brenda guarded Wanda, and I guarded Maye. We heard shots from Wanda's room, and I ran to her room to find Brenda. Wanda had it under control. Two of the intruders were dead, and one of our guards and Wanda was wounded.

"What? OMG, is Maye okay? Was she hurt? Did she shoot?"

"Sir, when we left, her IV was back in her arm, and she was asleep."

"Wait a minute! Back in her arm?"

"Sir, she and Wanda took them out for more mobility; they said it hindered their gun hand."

Ward laughed, seeing Frank run his fingers through his hair, saying, "Where are those forms for me to fill out? I might as well get started!"

"Sir, Maye didn't shoot her gun; Wanda did all the shooting!

Frank slumped back in his chair and would have been talked into lying down on the cot if the shooting hadn't started outside.

It wasn't much of a fight with all the backup, but you must give Clarence credit. He continued the assault even after he realized the cops had extra men with superior weapons. Most of his men were wounded and taken into custody.

Ward had Clarence brought to the task room for questioning, and he wasn't a happy man.

"Where in the hell did all those extra men come from? He screamed!"

"We scouted this building and knew how many people you had. Dammit! We could have taken you! Anyway, we got your girlfriend and Wanda," He started laughing hysterically until he saw the thunderous look on Frank's face.

Ward enjoyed telling him what had happened.

"Shit, that's what I get for hiring cheap help!"

Ward had him taken downstairs and put away from the other men in a cell.

He wanted to allow Frank to be present when he interrogated Clarence. Knowing Frank, he planned on the first interview for the next day.

He took Shirl and Brenda aside and suggested they take Frank home and make sure he stayed. "Do anything short of sitting on him; don't let him come back tonight!"

He agreed to go home on one condition: they take him to see Maye first.

Sitting by her bed, holding her hand, he couldn't wait for both of them to be able to sleep in their new home.

Reaching for the call button, his hand was stopped by Shirl. "Exactly what do you need a nurse for?

"I want to have a cot brought in to guard her. We might not have got all of Clarence's men."

"Good try, Frank, but we rounded up all of them, and you are going home to bed."

They walked him to the car, drove him to Maye's apartment, and put him to bed. He had about as much fight as Maye and was asleep before Brenda and Shirl tiptoed out of the room.

They made beds on the couch, not trusting him to stay in bed if they left.

"Brenda, don't you think wasting that great-looking king bed is a shame? Shirl said, getting brave enough to put his arms around her and kissing her neck.

"Shirl, sweetie, Frank has never officially rescinded his order to shoot you! He is not who you should be afraid of. Do you want to be the one who explains to Maye that you had sex in her new bed before she did?"

"But, if it weren't her new bed, would I have a chance?"

"Ask me again when the shooting stops." She said with a wink and a peck on his cheek.

Chapter 20 Maye comes home.

Frank woke the next morning to the smell of fresh coffee. He showered, dressed, and found Shirl and Brenda in the kitchen with his favorite Danish. They looked pretty satisfied with themselves.

"Hey, thanks, guys, this is great!" He said, sitting down, taking a big bite, and remarking that the coffee was perfect. "Did you guys sleep here?"

"We were given orders to bring you home, put you to bed, and sit on you if necessary. But not allow you back to the office until this morning.

"You can go home and be at the office when I return from checking on Maye and Wanda."

"Yes, Sir," they both said with grins.

Arriving at the hospital, he found Maye and Wanda up and dressed, waiting for a ride home. "Wait a minute, how did you talk the Doctor into letting you go home today?"

"Dr. Sorenson decided we would be safer at home and rest better in our beds. Of course, we didn't tell him Wanda doesn't have a bed; Maye laughed. She can have our spare bedroom. I can't wait to see what damage Lavonne has done to my office and home. Don't worry about us; Mary Anne will protect us."

Frank couldn't help smiling.

Wanda said, "I can't wait to meet her, but are you sure, Maye? I don't want to cramp your style. You know, you Honeymooners and all!"

Frank's face turned a little pink as they guffawed. Under protest and after checking with the Dr., he reluctantly drove them to Maye's office. He parked in front and tried to help them into the office. Wanda put her arm around Maye's waist and told him, "Get going; I can do this." And she would have, too, if Mary Anne hadn't rushed out and taken Maye's arm on the other side. Dismissed, Frank said "Goodbye" and headed for the office.

The girls headed for the break room, where Maye and Wanda sunk into chairs, declaring, "We can rest for a few minutes, and then I need to inspect the damage sweet Lavonne did to my home.

Mary Anne handed both of them coffee and sweet Blueberry muffins. She sat and said, "Alright, tell me everything!" How many did you kill, and who shot who?"

Frank arrived to find that Ward had been there since 6, setting up interviews with several of Clarence's men and Clarence for late afternoon. The guys shook hands, and Frank asked who they were interviewing first.

"We will start with the ones from the park assault, the hospital shooters, and Clarence by the end of the day."

They kept at it all day, and Ward only let up when his stomach started growling, matching Frank's. They discussed what to order when Shirl and Brenda arrived with Burgers, fries, and a frosty for everyone.

"Clarence's men have said hardly a word. I wonder what kind of hold he has over them to keep them silent?" Ward mused.

"Maybe if they keep quiet, they get a big payday," Brenda said.

"I'll bet he isn't nearly as good at hiding money as Wanda!" Shirl said.

"Has his business and home been searched?" Frank asked Ward.

"We thought of that, and his house and business were torn apart. We didn't find 20 cents!

"He has to have a stash somewhere. Maybe Wanda has an idea. I will question her tonight.

Brenda said, "If she knew where he kept a lot of money, wouldn't she have taken it when she ran? She could have only taken enough to get away and help Nate."

"If I was a paranoid man, where would I hide a lot of loot?" Shirl mused, "Hey, maybe he did the same thing Wanda did and hid it in a car! Do we know if he had a favorite vehicle? One he kept in great shape mechanically but looked like crap?

Everyone started shuffling papers, skim-reading; after several hours, Frank held up a paper and hollered, "Eureka!"

Ward looked at the paper and made a phone call. "We will have that car in our shop, and it will be taken apart piece by piece before morning. If there is money hidden, it will be here tomorrow. Once his men find they won't have a big payday for being loyal, they will cave."

Frank said, "I don't know about you guys, but I have had a long day, and Maye is waiting for me at our new home. The three women have been catching up at the office all afternoon. Maye won't admit it, but will be ready for our new hot tub and a soft bed. He called to ask what she wanted him to pick up and was told it was all arranged, to just come home. He said goodbye and disappeared! Leaving his friends with smiles on their faces.

Maye met him at the door; her eyes were sparkling like the wine in the two glasses in her hands. Gratefully taking one, he closed the door behind him.

Frank moved close and, taking the glass from her hand, folded her into his arms. They stood there, loving the feeling of their bodies touching. Maye stood on tiptoes as they kissed deeply; it had been ages since they were alone.

Pulling away, Maye said, "Hold on, big fella, we have a wonderful dinner waiting for us courtesy of Mary Anne and Wanda. Wanda, by the way, is spending the night with Mary Anne. We are alone." Taking his hand, she led him to the dining room. The table was set with Maye's best china, and the new chandelier gave the perfect romantic setting.

"I hope you won't be disappointed in the crab and cheddar dinner from Butches."

"It is perfect," Frank said, noticing her negligee. They enjoyed their meal, and Maye took his hand, leading him to the now-finished workout area with the hot tub bubbling. He noticed more wine cooling in the attached bucket.

"Woman, you know the way to a man's heart, but we need to be less encumbered. He slipped her nightie off her shoulders as she unbuttoned his shirt. Within minutes, they were naked. Pausing, noticing the bandage on her belly, asked, "Will this be okay?"

"Of course, I am not going to swim; just sit unless you have something else in mind," She said, looking up into his eyes and moving close enough to give him ideas. He mentally slapped himself to keep from doing what his mind and body were urging him to do. They slid into the bubbles, leaned back, looked up, and saw shooting stars through the large skylight.

Sipping the champagne, Maye had a thought. "We need to have a get-together to celebrate the new offices, Ed's semi-retirement, and anything else we can think of!"

"Great idea! We should close the case, and maybe I will take a few days off. We could quietly tie the knot and have a honeymoon."

"Lavonne will be so disappointed if she can't plan our wedding. But we could allow her to plan the reception. Or better yet, we could include it in the celebration.

Frank was thrilled to hear Maye talk about marriage and agreed it would be a good idea. He was more thrilled when Maye straddled his lap and moved close, slipping her arms around his neck. She began kissing him and moving her body suggestively against his until he couldn't stand it any longer. "Maye, honey, I am afraid of hurting you."

"Don't worry, I need you as much as you need me; it will be okay." She said in his ear, and they made slow, beautiful love in the tub.

They slept a little longer and woke slower, comfortable in the new bed. Frank remembered carrying Maye over the threshold of their new bedroom and smiled. He slid out of bed into his robe and made coffee in the new kitchen. Bringing a cup to Maye, he sat on the bed and looked at her for a few seconds before she woke to the smell of fresh coffee. Looking up, she smiled and said, "Is one of those for me?"

Chapter 21 Case closed and housewarming.

When Frank arrived at work, he found Ward in the garage with Clarence's getaway car. The crew had removed the exterior and were in the process of dismantling it piece by piece.

Frank said, "I have a suggestion for determining if the car holds the secrets we suspect. How about asking Clarence?"

Ward started laughing and said, "It might be fun whether it works or not! Frank had Clarence brought to an interview room and secured his hands to the desk. He asked a few preliminary questions, knowing Clarence would not answer. Clarence relaxed until Ward said. "We might as well have you taken back to your cell since you won't talk."

Clarence laughed, saying, "You will never get anything from me. Just wait, I will beat this rap! I've got friends in high places!"

"Yeah, we know, we saw their names in your books! By the way, is this your favorite car?" Frank said as he slid a picture across the desk. "Our mechanic noticed it was in excellent condition on the inside. The outside needs a little work. Was this your favorite car?"

Clarence's face turned several shades of red. "Dammit, you know it is! I did all the work on it myself. My ex thinks she is so friggin' smart! My baby would leave her cute little car in the dust!

"Too bad you couldn't test that theory."

"When I get outta here, I might just do that."

"You will have to put it back together because, as we speak, it is being taken apart."

"Ward, do you think we will find anything interesting?

"I don't know. Clarence, what do you think?"

Clarence's face became beet red as he struggled to get his hands out of the cuffs. The guys left him swearing like a pirate as they walked out and shut the door.

"That was a great idea! Clarence told us what we wanted to know. Let's go down to the garage to see what they found."

As they walked into the garage, they heard a mechanic saying, "Well, son of a bitch, I wouldn't have believed he was that clever." He was leaning into the engine cavity.

"There is no way he put anything into the engine cavity, but look at this. He didn't plan on ever cleaning his windshields; when we removed the reservoir, there was no sound of liquid sloshing, and it seemed quite heavy to be empty. It was two sizes bigger than the car needed. We found stacks of one thousand dollar bills packed neatly inside when we opened it."

"Has it been counted? Ward asked.

"No, we are concentrating on finding more empty places. We have taken the seat cushions, backs, and armrests apart. No more money there. We removed the door panels, and they had several plastic bags packed with bills."

As Ward and Frank watched, the crew removed the car's top and searched every nook and cranny. The rest of the crew were dismantling the floorboards and found more plastic bags packed with money. This continued for hours.

The garnered money was brought to the Task Force room and was given to officers to count. The process was filmed from several angles, from when the packages were uncovered through counting. The counters had just finished and announced $2,580,000.00 when another officer came in with two more plastic bags. $1,850,000. 00 was added, bringing the total to $4,430,000.00.

Ward enjoyed this much more than Frank thought he would, and he asked, "Do you want to make another run at Clarence today?

"Oh, yes, I believe in striking while the iron is hot, and Mr. Poole is pretty hot now."

Frank settled by the window, watching Ward casually walk into the room, drop a stack of thousand-dollar bills just out of Clarence's reach, and sit at the opposite end of the table.

"You son of a bitch! That's my money, you can't keep it. I earned it honestly working in my shop. You can't prove anything different! I didn't do anything wrong!"

"You can show books to justify this money from doing mechanic work out of your shop? Speaking of your shop, we now have a warrant to secure your records. We will look at the computer system Nate set up for you. He has agreed to help decipher it for us." This brought another string of blue language from Clarence. And more yanking on his wrist cuffs."

Fearing Clarence was damaging his wrists, Frank had him returned to his cell and had a Doctor bandage them. He placed a suicide watch on him, only to keep track of anyone going near his cell.

They met at the task room and sat over coffee discussing the case, waiting for the search of Clarence's garage. The time dragged slowly, and after several hours, Ward suggested Frank go home to check on Maye.

"We can have the search team contact us the minute they finish the search, and tomorrow, we will sort through everything."

"You may be right; I can use a rest. I have ordered a ring for Maye and will pick it up tomorrow. Last night, we agreed to get hitched on Saturday and let Lavonne plan a reception. We are afraid if we wait, Lavonne will plan an elaborate wedding, and we will go along with it because we both love her so much. Help me out, Ward. What do you think?"

I have only met Lavonne at the party at Butch's, but I think you are doing the right thing. Miss Lavonne will not be content with letting you go to a Justice of the Peace. Do either of you have any affiliation with a Church?"

"No, we go to church occasionally but don't want a big wedding. Just a few friends and a Minister will be just right."

"Buddy, have you picked your Best Man? He usually does all the footwork for you."

"I don't have anyone in mind; Shirl is as close to being a friend that I have, other than you. Since Shirl is under my command, it might cause hard feelings with the other men."

"I feel as close to you as I have allowed myself to be with co-workers. I would be honored to stand in as your Best Man. You and Maye talk it over; no worries if you have someone else in mind. Candy and I will be happy to help however we can."

Frank shook hands and said he would get back to him in the morning with an answer.

When Frank walked in, Wanda was in the kitchen, several pots simmering on the stove. The delicious aroma set Frank's stomach growling.

"Dinner is ready; if you don't mind waking up Maye, we can eat."

"Thanks, Wanda."

In a few minutes, they returned with appetites. "Jeb is planning on heading back to Texas. I was thinking of going with them if it would be okay. I promise to come back for the trial." Wanda said.

"I don't think it will be a problem; it will be months or years before it goes to trial."

"Do you know when they are leaving?" Maye asked.

"Jeb and John talked about later this week. John is anxious to take Lavonne home to Texas for a few weeks. She is caught up on her projects but plans to return later this year."

Maye and Frank looked at each other and smiled. Later, they discussed the wedding and agreed that Ward would be a great Best Man, and Maye said she wanted Lavonne as her maid of honor.

"She will never forgive me if she isn't part of our wedding. But we must have it all planned before letting her get involved. And we need to do it before the crew leaves for Texas. I will contact my florist and order flowers and Butch for the cake and a meal for everyone attending. You and Ward will have to plan the rest of it. I would like it in my new office. Just our closest friends."

"Maye, we will still have quite a few people." When they finished their list, there were more than 20 people.

"I would love to take you someplace exotic...I interrupted him with a kiss, saying, "It doesn't matter where we go. We will be together. I am getting used to having you around. Let's plan on Saturday afternoon for the ceremony. Can you guys get everything ready? I will talk to Lavonne and maybe let her come with me to pick out my outfit and her dress. Can I borrow your extra pair of handcuffs?"

Frank laughed as he pulled me close and kissed me.

The next morning, Frank and Maye told Wanda about the wedding, and she was thrilled to be invited and asked what she could do to help.

"Today, I am going to contact Butches Restaurant to have him cater the reception and will need to pick out flowers. We can check out several Bridal shops and pick out dresses for Lavonne and me. You could go along if you would like and help me keep Lavonne in check. Frank wouldn't let me have a pair of handcuffs!"

Wanda was giggling when she placed a call to Jeb to inform them about a Saturday wedding. Maye could hear Lavonne shriek, demanding that she speak to Maye.

"Maye, I will be part of this, won't I?" She said.

"Yes, sweetie, you will be my Maid of Honor unless you don't want to." I quickly moved the phone away from my ear to preserve my hearing.

"Hon, we have everything about planned. I am calling Butch to have him cater, and Wanda and I are going to David's Bridal shop; you can come with us if you want to." More shrieking followed. "I will be there in an hour. Don't you dare to leave without me!" Wanda and I nearly spit out our coffee laughing.

We went downstairs to tell Mary Anne the news and invited her.

"Maye, it has been several days since you came home, and I have wanted to show you an addition to the plans we didn't have time to discuss. It may make your party with the number of people you mentioned less intimate." She led them to the reception area next to the kitchen break room.

"Watch this!" Mary Anne said. She slid the entire wall separating the reception from the kitchen to the north wall. Suddenly, they were standing in a large enough room for the 20 quests to be fed and room to dance, too!

"OMG! I didn't even think about this when I was planning the expansion. Whose idea was this? Yours?"

"No, I wish it was; it was Al and Mich's brainchild. You were so busy with other things I gave them the go-ahead to make the changes. I hope it is okay."

"Okay! It is fantastic! Thank you." I grabbed her in a bear hug until I realized what I was doing. This was not me, and by the look on her face, she was startled but pleased. *"I have to get myself under control; this wedding thing is making me do crazy things! Damn! When this week ends, maybe things will return to normal."*

"Is there anything else you added that I should know about? I said with a straight face.

"No, I figured that was enough." She looked so unsure, I laughed and said, "I love it!"

We were sitting in the new break room with coffee, talking about the wedding, when Lavonne breezed in. Grabbing me in a tight hug, exclaiming how excited she was to be part of my wedding. *"Now I was worried!"*

"Now, Lavonne, you understand, we want a simple ceremony, nothing elaborate! Right?"

"Of course! Your wish is my command!" She said, with a smart salute and a pleased-as-punch look. *"I not only have been assimilated, but I am on the Mother ship on the way to her home planet!"*

"Mary Anne, if you hold down the office for the morning, we will come back and take you to Butches for lunch! We will be looking at dresses for Lavonne and me at David's Bridal Shop. We will stop by the florist to look at the arrangements. We will make it a late lunch and probably call it a day. I still need my nap in the afternoon."

"Anything I can do for you?"

"Yes, call Mitch, invite the family, and tell her how much I love the addition. If you would like, you can create invitations for me. We can have them hand-delivered or by email. Text me if you have any questions. Frank and I do not have any relatives, so it should be simple."

"I will have several for you to look at by the time you pick me up. Do you think Butch will flirt with all of us?"

"I guarantee it!"

I am surprised Lavonne didn't have us three girls, arm in arm, skipping out the door. I have to admit, we had a great time, and the suggestions of Wanda and Lavonne made my anxiety fade away. I was left with a feeling of fun and adventure. Between the good taste of Lavonne and Wanda, we found a beautiful dress for me. It was simple but elegant. Lavonne's, of course, was elegant, also. She kept it simple, probably so she would not outshine the bride. But Lavonne would be beautiful in a burlap sack.

At the florist, we ran into trouble. Wanda was the voice of reason between Lavonne's lavish arrangements and the simple ones I liked. Once the decision was made, I suggested we pick up Mary Anne, which was met with approval. That was good, as I was starting to fade a little.

Wanda offered to be chauffeur, but I called a limo, and we arrived in style. Butch met us at the door and escorted us to one of his larger alcoves. In seconds, we had champagne glasses and a magnum in the ice bucket!.

"And what would you ladies like to have today?" He said.

Lavonne said, "I want medium-rare steak and lobster!" "*I don't know how a tiny person can eat so much and never gain a pound!*" The rest of the girls followed suit, so I indulged too! After all, a girl doesn't get married that many times in her life!

Butch was his usual adorable self, and we giggled as he flirted with all of us. Lavonne and I enjoyed watching the reaction of Mary Anne and Wanda. Suddenly, Mary Anne said, "OMG, I have left the office closed all afternoon!"

"No worries. Butch has our leftovers packed, and the limo is waiting. Let's stop at the office and have coffee."

"There is nothing for you to worry about, Maye. Frank's Best Man, Ward, and I will care for everything." Said my devious little Maid of Honor.

Butch escorted us to the limo. He placed our leftovers in the trunk, and we went to my office.

I admitted I was beat and allowed Frank to take me upstairs and put me to bed while the girls had coffee and made plans for what they assured me I would approve.

Frank allowed me to sleep in. He slid out of bed, showered, and left for the office before I opened my eyelids. I showered and dressed for work. Entering the kitchen, I found Wanda sitting at the table with a cup of coffee. She jumped up, poured one for me, and refilled her cup.

"What would you like for breakfast?" she asked.

"I don't know. Are there any muffins left?"

"Maye, I can cook, and I am hungry, and I waited for you so we could talk."

"You don't have to wait on me. But scrambled eggs and toast would be great if you are eating too."

"Coming up; how about some bacon or ham, too?"

Within minutes, sitting before me was a wonderful omelet of ham, cheese, and mushrooms.

"What? I had to eat too!" Wanda smiled behind her identical plate.

We enjoyed our food, and before I could interrogate her, she told me they reined in Lavone between her and Mary Anne. They kept the flowers and food simple but elegant. She insisted Lavonne leave a sketch of what she dreamed up for my wedding. I breathed a sigh of relief when I saw them. They were wonderful.

On the other hand, Frank was up to his eyebrows in problems. He arrived with coffee and a Danish, hoping to enjoy it before diving in. Ward was waiting, and grudging allowed him time to gulp down coffee and scarf the Danish.

"Clarence's lawyer showed up this morning and is in a private conference room with him. We will talk with the honorable Floyd Jenkins as soon as they finish."

"Just what I need today. What does Mr. Jenkins think he can do for Clarence? He still has several years on his conviction of trying to kill his wife. We will add so many years on top of that. He will have a life sentence!" Frank steamed.

"I understand, but we have to humor him. We don't want to be guilty of any offense that can be used against us. We will listen to his proposal and let our attorneys handle the aftermath. It should be fun hearing what he will try to pull. We need to keep a straight face."

When the honorable Floyd Jenkins emerged from his conference with Clarence, he looked like he had the world's weight on his shoulders.

He shook hands with Frank and thanked Ward for the time to confer with his client. Frank invited him to follow them to the conference room. The three men sat around the table, and Frank asked if he would like coffee or tea, and he said no. Floyd was all business in his stylish suit, Dunhill Belgrave leather attache case, and a dour expression. He was shorter than either of the men, and his hair was short and ice-white, contrasting with the blackness of his sharp little eyes.

"Mr. Jenkins, does your client wish to make a statement and confess his guilt?" Ward asked.

"No, I am afraid Clarence is unrepentant. He thinks he will be able to prove that this action was justified by his ex-wife's theft of his business books!"

"Did he tell you that he and several dozen mercenaries attacked the Phoenix Sheriff's building?" Frank asked.

"No, he said he was trying to negotiate the release of his personal property and was fired upon by your deputies. In self-defense, he and his men returned fire. Of course, with the additional FBI manpower, he was overcome." Mr. Jenkins said with a serious look on his face. Before either Ward or Frank could speak, he continued. "Mr. Poole further contends that he sent emissaries to the hospital merely to secure his ex-wife's signature on their final divorce papers and property settlement. She shot and killed both of them without cause."

"Mr. Jenkens, off the record, I hope you are well paid because there isn't a chance of a snowball in China that he will be able to slip out of this. We have well-documented proof and witness of his guilt." Ward said.

"I am filing charges and will require copies of your proof for verification before trial. We will request that all witnesses remain in this jurisdiction to be available for depositions."

"We will cooperate and will expect cooperation in return. Many of Clarence's mercenaries have been arraigned and charged and will remain behind bars until trial. Clarence will be returned to Florence prison and remain locked until his trial for the rest of the charges we will be filing." Ward said without a raise in his voice.

Everyone shook hands, and as soon as Mr. Jenkens was out the door, Frank and Ward leaned back in their chairs and laughed until tears rolled down their faces. "My God, was he serious? I wonder what Clarence has on him? His name didn't appear in the books that Wanda hid from Clarence. It must be big! I think I will have my investigators look into him and his family quietly. As a matter of fact, his whole firm might need some surveillance. " His face looked thunderous.

"Ward, remind me never to piss you off!"

"No worries. It's time we pressure the mercenaries to see if we can get some roll-over." They spent the better part of the day attempting to do just that. By dinner time, they realized the grapevine had been faster than anticipated, and they wouldn't talk. Frank and Ward decided to head home.

Chapter 22 Wedding jitters.

By the end of the week, I started to feel more like myself and had given up the afternoon naps. Frank asked me to go to dinner on Thursday night. He wouldn't tell me where we were going. He picked me up in a limo and whisked me away for a romantic evening. There was champagne chilled in an ice bucket and a shrimp cocktail to snack on. It felt like we were alone in the universe.

I could feel the limo climbing the hill overlooking Phoenix. Frank took my glass and set it down as he slid off the seat with one knee on the floor.

"Maye, I loved you from the minute we first met and was afraid you would never agree to marry me. I have been carrying this around for months, trying to get the courage to ask you to be my wife."

Reaching into his pocket, he took out a small heart-shaped box; opening it, he said, "Maye West, will you accept this ring and make me the happiest man alive?"

He looked so pathetic, and I was speechless for several minutes. When I finally breathed, I said, "Mr. Singleton, I will be honored to be your lover for the rest of my life."

I let him put a beautiful matching wedding and engagement ring on my finger, slid off the couch, and put my arms around his neck. We kissed, and the world stood still.

We had an amazing dinner at The Top of the Hill under the twinkling stars and the lights of Phoenix! When the Limo brought us home, we weren't sorry Wanda found another bed for the night.

Friday started like any other day; things changed when I descended to my office. Mary Anne greeted me with a stack of papers for me to review.

Within minutes, a cup of coffee and a muffin were placed in front of me.

"I'll bet you didn't have breakfast, right?"

"Yes, my cook disappeared last night. You didn't have anything to do with that, did you?"

"I found her a room at one of those in-suites. She told me that she was uncomfortable staying with your honeymooners. This way, she can check out any time if she decides to return to Texas. Wait a minute, hold that left hand still so I can get a look at that rock! Maye, that is beautiful!"

"Thanks. There is a matching band, too, but I thought I should wait until after the ceremony to wear both."

"Where are you going on your honeymoon?"

"I don't think we are going anywhere. Frank is wound up in the Poole case, and I have new agents to train. One, in particular, Michael York, will take most of my time. He thinks he is a hotshot and a ladies' man, and he is neither. I need to keep him on a short lease. He will cut corners if he thinks he can get away with it. Now, I would like to have a dozen like George Peterson's! He is a retired broker, just in the game to keep busy. Sarah McClanahan is also a dream agent. She does a ton of rural listings and sales, her paperwork is perfect, and she is unfazed by the strange profession of Real Estate. Last year, finding the owners of a new listing dead with crossbow bolts in their chests didn't make her quit. Frank was impressed by how she handled it.

"Between Ed McGinley and me, we can handle the office; you could sneak away for a few days, at least, couldn't you?"

"I don't know; it depends on how the Poole case goes."

"But surely, Ward can handle everything."

"I am sure he can, but will Frank let him?" Their discussion was interrupted by the arrival of Butch to confirm how many people he would be feeding. "Maye, darlin', tell me it isn't true! You aren't going to marry that Fred fella, are you?" He said in his most pathetic voice.

"Only because you had cold feet and never asked me! You are too late! He has me corraled, and after Saturday, we both will have to grieve together at our champagne lunches."

"If you insist on going through with it, at least I can make the meal the best part of the evening! Now, how many are attending, other than me?"

"Let me get the guest list out, and we can go over it together. Lavonne is my Maid of Honor, and her fiance is John Kinney. Ward is Frank's Best Man, and Candy Stone is his wife. James Crandal and Vivian Appleton, Jeb Hanford, his pilot George, Al and Mitch Harris, Nate, Naomi, and Amanda Harris, Wanda Poole, Mary Anne Noble, Shawn, and Marielle McGarrett, Mi and Josh Feldman, Ed and Kaye McGinley, Shirl Packard, Brenda Brannen, Chet Fields, Martha Rehnquist, Max, and Margery Snell, George Peterson, Michael York, Fred Potts, Marshall, and Margery Soderman, and Sarah McClanahan."

"That is 33 total guests and a wedding party. That should be no problem; my wait staff has volunteered to serve. Will this one be Western-style, or are you going traditional?"

I brought out the sketches Lavonne had thoughtfully left, and he looked them over. "Maye, how will you get everyone in the break or the reception room?"

"The wall between them will slide out of the way to make one large room. Mary Anne will show you before you leave how it works."

"Do you already have a volunteer bartender, or should I bring mine?"

"I have several friends that could stand in, but I would like my guests to enjoy themselves, so bring your bartender. Clarence and his minions are in jail, so there is little chance of encountering any problems. Many of my guests are law enforcement, so we will be protected."

"That is good to know, darling, but are you sure you want to marry that Fred guy? Will he object to our afternoon trysts?"

"No, sweetie, he will not mind, and I will try to bring Mary Anne and occasionally Lavonne when she is in town." He sighed and asked me to show him how the wall receded. When I released the lever and the wall slid back, the two rooms became one large area, and he twirled around, marveling at the transformation.

"This is amazing! I love it! I need to talk to the Harris'. I have an idea of some renovations. I have put a bid on an adjoining property. I have considered adding a reception area for weddings and other formal occasions. The library will still be yours, anytime you want." He said, seeing the look on my face.

"Good, we have had so many wonderful times there; I would be lost without it."

Butch breezed out, and Frank entered with burgers, fries, and frostys. He allowed me to enjoy my lunch before he told me the latest Poole news.

"Maye, Clarence apparently tried to commit suicide last night. He slashed his wrists and partially hanged himself.

"What?" I thought he was put on suicide watch? How could that happen?"

"The guards were distracted by an inmate fight in the exercise yard. He was found before he was successful."

"Define successful? How bad is he?"

"He bled a lot, and he appears to be having trouble breathing."

"Appears to? Do you think he is faking?"

"I don't know. The Doctor said the cuts on his wrists weren't deep enough to require surgery. His breathing is debatable. There is some bruising, but we don't think he suffered any permanent effects. Ward is keeping him under guard while we are away. Let's not worry about him! From this moment on, we are only concentrating on tomorrow."

"Tomorrow? What is so special about tomorrow?" I said.

"You know what! I will finally marry you and spend the rest of my life with you."

"Well, if you insist."

"I do."

"If Lavonne gets her way, we both might wish we had run away."

"What more could she plan? She has me in a tux and has decorated your office with so many flowers it will look like a flower shop!"

"Tomorrow morning, she will kick you out, and you won't be able to come back until time for the wedding. Your best man is in on it! He will be her enforcer!"

"Tell me about it! I had to practically pull my gun for her to let me stay with you tonight. She gave me marching orders: I can't see you in your dress until you walk down the aisle. Maye, there isn't an aisle for you to walk down. Will one mysteriously appear?"

"You know Lavonne as well as I do. What do you think?"

"As long as you don't mind, I don't either. I just want to put those rings on your finger and say I do forever."

"I kinda like that...

"Kinda? I will have to prove that you will more than kinda like it?

And he did a lovely job convincing me that I would love having those rings on my fingers.

The next morning, true to her word, Lavonne was at our door and almost threw Frank out! Ward and Shirl were waiting downstairs for him to emerge. They scooped him up, and off they went for a day of adult male playtime. Lavonne warned Ward and Shirl that they had better get Frank to the church on time; of course, the church was my newly finished and decorated office.

She would not let me go down and look at anything! The minute I was dressed, she allowed me a light breakfast. Wanda and Viv arrived and dragged me off for a spa day. I have to admit, it was fun being pampered for several hours. By the time I had a full body massage, hair trim, facial, and pedi/manicure, I was ready for lunch. We thought about Butches, but he would be busy getting food ready, so we stopped at the recovery room for lunch and wine.

"It was fun re-telling the girls about Frank and George Greens' escapade. Viv loved the story's retelling, and Wanda laughed, picturing

Frank drunk. We were having a second glass when Viv's phone rang. She said, "Okay, Yes, and Will do."

"Let me guess, that was Lavonne."

"Yes, and we need to book! We have to have you dressed in one hour."

We arrived at my apartment, and the girls helped me get dressed. They wouldn't let me go downstairs until everything was ready. I have to admit it was a beautiful wedding, the decorations were wonderful. I always wonder how Lavonne does it! She is a little slip of a thing and a whirlwind when she is decorating."

I will always remember the look on Frank's face when I appeared and walked toward him. After the ceremony, the reception was extraordinary, considering my poor Lavonne's time planning and executing the arrangements.

Frank and I were speechless when Jeb surprised us with his and Evie's wedding present. Jeb gave us the keys to his Condo in Hawaii! He had George fly us there and come pick us up a week later. His wife Evie arranged several things to please us!

We had a wonderful honeymoon, and it was over too soon, and we came home to start our future together.

Don't miss out!

Visit the website below and you can sign up to receive emails whenever Brenda Colbath publishes a new book. There's no charge and no obligation.

https://books2read.com/r/B-A-GZMG-KTWLB

BOOKS 2 READ

Connecting independent readers to independent writers.

Did you love *Options*? Then you should read *Spirited One*[1] by Brenda Colbath!

[2]

The cover of Spirited One might appear to be a ghost story, but it is a Fantasy, Sci-Fi, and fiction. Orphaned at age one, Jena Andrews grew up in the Foster System. She accepted her lot in life, understanding it would never be easy. Anger issues thrust her into court-appointed therapy to remember the horror hidden in her mind's deepest recesses. It only re-visits her in the dead of night, waking every morning in sweat-soaked sheets, screaming! Her life consists of teaching Taekwondo, 5-mile runs, and waitressing at Olive Garden! A new student joins her beginners' class, and she meets her new therapist, plus the Spirited One, who changes her life forever! Why was she chosen by the Spirited One? What is the Spirited One?

1. https://books2read.com/u/318zPv

2. https://books2read.com/u/318zPv

Also by Brenda Colbath

Book 1
Spirited One

Maye West Murder Mysteries
Murder on Lake Haverly
Options

The Spirited One
James Book 2

About the Author

Creating worlds and characters and wielding power like a madwoman makes my characters happy, sad, angry, and have no redeeming qualities. I laugh aloud when writing a scene, and I have been known to cry when one of my favorites dies.

I am a left-handed Gemini; what do you expect?

Read more at https://wordpress.com/stats/day/ brendacolbathbooks.com.